Bait and Switch

Blythe H. Warren

BELLA
BOOKS

2017

Bella Books, Inc.
P.O. Box 10543
Tallahassee, FL 32302

Printed in the United States of America on acid-free paper.

First Bella Books Edition 2017

Editor: Ann Roberts
Cover Designer: Sandy Knowles

ISBN: 978-1-59493-565-7

Other Bella Books by Blythe H. Warren

My Best Friend's Girl

Acknowledgments

I never would have considered writing this book if not for the friends I found in college—Ellen Joyce, Heather Mathes, Kris Fahey Nelson and the rest of our small, strange group, I learned as much through our friendship as I did in my classes (and being the good kid, I learned *a lot* in my classes). In particular, I am indebted to Fahey for giving me the idea for this book. It was one of the most challenging and satisfying writing experiences I've had so far, so thank you for giving me this opportunity. Thanks also to Eve Barrs for answering my questions about fishes and the life of an aquarist. You shared far more than I could write down. Even better, you helped me recapture my love for the aquarium. As always, I'm grateful for the support, encouragement, patience, feedback and prodding of my sisters Jennie Tyderek and Heidi Krystofiak (my Knowledge Sherpa and Professional Nag, respectively). To my partner, Sue Hawks, you talked me up from my self-doubt more times than I can count, and you are the perfect sounding board when my characters refuse to behave. I'm blessed to have you. My beta readers—Amy Cook, Kathy Rowe, Erin Dunn, Jamie Lee Winner, Rory Rowe, Lynda Fitzgerald, Diane Piña and HLM— thank you for making this a better book, and thank you for doing it so kindly. Additional thanks to the staff at Monk's (especially Cheryl, Anthony and Beth) for plying me with beer and (along with fellow patron Tyler Ventura) offering title suggestions, and to Diane—you can name all my books from this point forward. To my amazing editor, Ann Roberts, you challenged me to be a better writer, and though I didn't always enjoy it, I definitely appreciate it. Finally, to everyone at Bella—I'm honored and proud to put my work in your hands. Thank you for all you do.

About the Author

Blythe H. Warren teaches English to college freshman, and she has a terrible reputation for infecting English-weary composition haters with her love of writing. They enter her class dreading the written word and leave thinking that writing can actually be fun. When she is not busy writing or shamelessly converting young minds, she enjoys (yes, actually enjoys) running marathons. Much to her surprise, her first book *My Best Friend's Girl* was nominated for a Lammy and a Goldie. She and her partner live in Chicago with their pets.

Dedication

For the young women of Pemberton Hall, 1994–1996.
Your support and friendship were more than any gay girl
in the nineties could have hoped for. Love, Edge

CHAPTER ONE

"Ollie?"

My stomach fell, and my head snapped in the direction of the voice. I had no idea who had spoken, but I was certain I wouldn't be happy to find out. No one had called me Ollie in the last fifteen years. Well, no one other than Patsy Collins, my best friend, but she never let anything go. A decade and a half after college ended she was still milking jokes that had amused her back then.

But Patsy also knew how much I hated that nickname, so she only used it when she was upset with me, which happened often thanks to my pig-headed stubborn side—her words, not mine. Since it was eight thirty on a Saturday morning—almost pre-dawn for my night-owl friend—it couldn't be Patsy using my old nickname. But who was it?

Craning my neck, I tried to scan the crowd inconspicuously. I was surrounded mostly by children—the almost twenty young girls who had been my students for the past week. They were now milling about the lobby of the aquarium where I worked as a marine biologist and where we had all spent the night. Whenever the opportunity arose, I tried to spearhead our educational efforts by teaching classes to every group that showed an interest. I've had senior citizens, scout troops, kindergarten classes and just about everything in between in my classroom, but this was the first time I'd designed and offered a course specifically for young girls. The verdict on the course was still out, but I hoped it had been successful enough for a repeat the following summer.

The girls (not even a little tired after an entire night of gossiping and pranking one another) were giggling, hugging, swapping phone numbers and saying goodbye as their parents gathered sleeping bags and backpacks, trying to herd their daughters in the direction of the exit. I didn't immediately recognize any of the parents as anyone who would think to call me Ollie.

Very few people knew my old nickname. I wasn't wildly popular in college, even before circumstances forced me out of the dorms. While there was a chance that the voice belonged to one of the rare friendly faces from my days in undergrad, given my luck over the last twenty-four hours, I felt confident this wouldn't be a joyful reunion. I mean, why wouldn't a horrible reliving of my hellish college years come at the tail end of a day that had already included an abruptly cold shower (jarring even in mid-summer), no drinkable caffeine in my apartment, a flat tire on my bike and Carson Phillips (one of my students) suffering through a serious asthma attack without her inhaler? Obviously that last one was worse for Carson than it was for me. I'd just kept the situation under control until the paramedics arrived to help her, but the anxiety I felt in those endless, terror-stricken minutes before help arrived was enough to turn even the most stoic person into a nervous wreck.

As I looked tentatively about for the source of this unwanted bit of nostalgia, I heard it again. "Ollie? Is that you?" Something vaguely familiar about the voice tugged at my memory as I continued to scan the crowd. Still seeing nothing, I hoped I was in the clear, and then my eyes locked on *her*, the source of almost all the torment in my life, my arch nemesis—Mira Butler.

Okay, maybe arch nemesis was a bit dramatic. It wasn't like we were in a comic book—Mira set to destroy Chicago with her super high-powered death ray unless I stopped her wicked plan. Certainly she could be a menace, but her reign of terror tended to be emotional and personal rather than physical. Somewhat less destructive (but no less evil) than obliterating the city, she was headed my way at warp speed, her expression one of oblivious good cheer. By the looks of her, she had no clue I despised her. That, or she had moved on.

In truth, I thought I had too. Even though she'd ruined my life, it wasn't like I'd spent the last fifteen years plotting sweet revenge. I had forgotten all about what she'd done, or so I thought. But seeing her there in my aquarium, beaming as she weaved in and out of clumps of chattering girls and earnest parents on her way to the spot where I stood, feet stubbornly glued to the earth that refused to open up and swallow me whole, brought back all of the hurt and anger and embarrassment from the humiliation she'd orchestrated. It felt as raw at that moment as it had more than fifteen years earlier.

Panicked, I searched for a way out of this encounter, but damn if every one of my students (who not an hour earlier had been clamoring for my attention) wasn't busy saying hello to parents or goodbye to classmates. I was on my own.

I just stood there, blinking stupidly and praying this was a vivid nightmare. Meanwhile, the closer a broadly grinning Mira got to me, the more I lost hope that I was still asleep. My system threatened to shut down as the very real possibility of a warm, friendly hug from my enemy grew larger, especially if I continued to stand there, silent and idle.

When I finally regained the power of speech, I blurted out the first thing I could think to say. "I don't go by Ollie anymore."

Her megawatt smile dimmed a kilowatt or two, and she put on the brakes far enough away that she couldn't manage an embrace, but unfortunately still close enough to converse.

"I'm sorry," she said, and she looked genuinely apologetic. "I didn't know." She waited a beat, possibly expecting me to reply, probably with what she should call me in place of Ollie. When I said nothing, she picked up the slack. "You look great."

That was a lie. I looked like I'd spent the night in an aquarium with nineteen adolescent girls. Without needing to check a mirror for confirmation, I knew that my usually uncooperative short hair stuck out in all directions like it was sending out distress signals. I didn't even want to think about the bags under my bloodshot eyes.

Mira, on the other hand, looked fantastic. Her long dark hair had that perfectly tousled look that comes from too much time and money spent in a salon. With her pillowy lips, large eyes and sculpted brows, I doubted Bernini could have formed a more perfect face, except for her nose. It was maybe a sliver too small, but I doubted anyone had ever complained. Her flawless beauty hadn't changed much in the fifteen years since I saw her last. It was depressing but not unexpected.

"What are you doing here?" I managed to sound more inquisitive than accusatory because she beamed again.

"I'm picking up my daughter," she said, and my heart sank as I watched Cassie Morgan, my favorite student, heading our way.

I knew I shouldn't have a favorite, and I was pretty sure I had managed to keep my preference a secret from everyone, but how could I help but adore Cassie? Her sharp mind and inquisitive nature energized everyone in the class. I should have expected as much because, on the first day of the course, she introduced herself to me before class and let me know that she was the vice president of the science club at her school and how excited she was to be learning from "a fellow woman of science."

As if that wasn't enough, she told me all this in sign language without preamble or comment on the fact that she was deaf. It reminded me of my mother, who maneuvered through life as a deaf woman in much the same way people with green eyes would, in other words, not worrying what those who weren't green eyed (or deaf) thought about the matter. For my mom, anyone who thought a hearing impairment was an issue or a handicap wasn't worth her time, and I got the impression that Cassie had a similar worldview. I pretty much fell in love with the kid right then and there. She was a science loving miniature version of my mom. No one else stood a chance.

Now here she was, embracing a woman I couldn't hate more if I tried. I stared at them, noting their physical similarities—dark hair, dark eyes, stunning smile—and prayed, in defiance of overwhelming visual evidence to the contrary, that Mira was not Cassie's mother. Or that Cassie had been adopted. Barring that, I hoped Mira had changed since college. It seemed both impossible and unfair that someone as sweet and wonderful as Cassie could have someone as close-minded and horrible as Mira Butler for a mother. Seeing them together, though, I had to admit that Cassie looked happy to be with her mom, so maybe Mira wasn't as evil as I remembered.

As I continued to stare and tell myself that Cassie wasn't fated to be a she-devil just because of her unfortunate lineage, Cassie signed something to her mother that I missed. I moved to step away and give them their privacy when Mira spoke.

"So you're Miss Liv," she said, recognition dawning.

"Guilty as charged, I guess."

"When Cassie hasn't been telling me about fish and ecosystems, she's been raving about Miss Liv. I was eager to meet my daughter's new favorite person. I had no idea I already knew her."

I couldn't help my snort, but based on her grin it came off as more of a "life is funny" guffaw than the "as if you actually know me" I'd been feeling when it slipped out.

"Small world," I said before Cassie handed me a pair of envelopes Mira had pulled from her purse.

Some of the other girls had already given me cards or even small gifts, so I wasn't caught completely off guard, but that didn't make me any less uncomfortable. I was glad they enjoyed the class enough to thank me, but that wasn't why I'd created the course. I just wanted the girls to learn about science, have fun while doing it and maybe see it as an option in their futures—or at least not dread the mandatory science classes they would face in school.

I signed a quick thanks and goodbye to Cassie before my embarrassment got the better of me, and I bid farewell to Mira, thinking I was fortunate to escape before she suggested we get together to catch up. With any luck this would be our last encounter.

Once all the girls cleared out and I had a moment to myself, I opened the tokens they had given me. Most had opted for pre-printed thank you cards in which they'd written short notes in their adorably bubbly cursive. I was also now the proud owner of three *World's Greatest Teacher* pencil holders and a planter shaped like a goldfish.

Cassie, whose cards I'd saved for last, had given me a thank you as well as an invitation to her thirteenth birthday party, taking place in one week. Perfect. Unless I wanted to disappoint a young girl I adored and admired, I would have to willingly spend more quality time with the woman who had accused me of rape.

Now what was I supposed to do?

CHAPTER TWO

I was a menace on two wheels all the way home thanks to my inability to focus on anything other than the unexpected invitation to Cassie's birthday party. While I was touched and honored she wanted me to be a part of her celebration, I was also alarmed. I was almost forty years old. How weird would it be to attend a thirteen-year-old's birthday party?

On top of the strangeness of going to a party where my only friend would be a child, there was the small matter of me hating her mother. Not an hour prior, I had implored the fates to keep me away from Mira from that point on. Now I was voluntarily contemplating another encounter in a week's time.

Reeling from that disturbing and distracting thought, I focused my commute just in time to avoid plowing into a pedestrian. When I swerved, I narrowly missed colliding with a parked car. This was not good, especially since I had already had two close encounters with cabs.

I eventually made it home (no closer to making a decision about Cassie's party but thankfully without breaking myself or my bike) and put the kettle on for a much-needed cup of tea. While foraging in my kitchen for something to eat, I called the one person who had seen me through every crisis in the last fifteen years.

"How was sleeping with the fishes?" Patsy asked.

"Fun but exhausting." I spotted a slightly dusty can of SpaghettiOs lurking in the back of a cabinet. "I think the girls got a lot out of it," I said, sparing her all the rotten details of my day. I didn't think she would want to hear about them any more than I wanted to relive them. Instead, I told her about the invitation from Cassie.

"Is she the one you've been raving about for days?"

"I might have mentioned her in passing." It wasn't like I'd spent all my free time singing Cassie's praises.

"Liv, you've brought her up at least once every time we've talked in the last week. I know more about this girl than I do my own family. I could buy her the perfect birthday present, and I've never met her. That's how much you've told me about her." Perhaps I'd been less restrained when it came to Cassie than I thought. "I think you should go to the party," Patsy advised. "She obviously likes you, and it's clear the feeling is mutual."

"There is a slight complication."

"Which is?"

"Aside from me being almost three times as old as the birthday girl, I know her mother."

"Oh my god, did you sleep with this kid's mom?"

"Gross," I shrieked, unsettled by the thought. "Not in a million years."

"You don't need to get so defensive. The way you get around, it's a wonder you haven't seduced more mothers."

"You're hilarious," I said. "And one to talk. Wreck any homes lately?" I knew she wouldn't be upset by my comment. She didn't quibble about little things like marital status when she considered sleeping with someone. It wasn't her fault if someone ignored his (or her) wedding vows. While I couldn't so easily facilitate adultery, I could see her point. They weren't her vows to uphold.

"The weekend is still young," she laughed. "What's the problem with Cassie's mother?"

"She's Mira Butler."

"Oh, shit."

That said it all, I thought as I watched my lunch spinning and bubbling in the microwave. "How can the coolest kid I've ever met come from the worst person I've ever known?"

"Oh, shit," Patsy said again, unable or unwilling to move past her shock.

"What should I do?" I whined.

"I can't decide for you, but I think you should go."

"Really?" I didn't know which answer I thought I'd get from her, but I had expected her to take at least a minute to ponder my dilemma.

"After all she's put you through, she owes you at least a piece of birthday cake."

"You're not really helping, you know." The microwave beeped, but I ignored my food, my appetite suddenly gone. "If you think I'm willingly going to subject myself to Mira Butler's brand of evil in exchange for some baked goods, you have lost your mind."

"In all seriousness, I think you should go."

"Why?" I sounded petulant to my own ears.

"You've obviously had an impact on this girl which, if I'm not mistaken, was what you set out to do when you dreamed up this class. It would be a shame to deprive Cassie of your mentorship just because her mother is a world-class asshole."

As usual, Patsy had hit the mark. It made her a great school counselor and perpetual sounding board. It would be irritating, if not for the fact that I so regularly needed her input.

"What about Mira?"

"Avoid her."

"That'll be easy at her daughter's birthday party."

"Just ask to sit at the kids' table. The conversation will probably be more interesting, and you won't have to worry about your deplorable table manners."

"That's very helpful. Thank you for your input." I knew I was being whiny and ungrateful, but I couldn't help it.

"The way you're acting now, you'll fit right in." I deserved that, but before I could apologize for being so bratty, she moved on. "What do you do when a guy hits on you?"

"On the rare occasion when that happens, I come out, but Mira already knows I'm gay. And unless you consider fabricating a tale of felony sexual assault a positive thing, she didn't react well to that news. I don't want to go down that road again."

"You know, she'll probably be too busy hosting the party to harass you. Just go and make the best of it."

"You're right," I said, not at all convinced that I could make the best of it or that I was even willing to try.

CHAPTER THREE

I let most of the week pass before I made a decision about Cassie's birthday party. In part I could blame my foot dragging on work. Construction on a new wing where we planned to house a series of special exhibits had fallen behind schedule. While construction delays were nothing new, these setbacks stretched our already thin budget even further and treated everyone to an extra helping of stress. Though fundraising and finances didn't typically fall under an aquarist's regular responsibilities, my boss Roman Singh (under immense pressure from the board) decided to take an "all hands on deck" approach to this particular crisis.

He wanted all of us acting as rainmakers in order to cover the deficit. I couldn't have been less qualified for a task if he'd asked me to molt or spontaneously combust. What could I even do? Host a fundraiser with my one friend in attendance? My contributions to this cause seemed hopeless, so every morning, I met his expectant grin with a frown and a dispirited shake of my head. I avoided him all day long and ended each day wanting nothing more than to drink a beer, shut off my brain and fall into bed. Planning my social calendar and calling Mira to RSVP seemed like too much effort.

That's the excuse I allowed myself anyway, but it was only half the story. In my more honest moments, I could admit that, really, I just didn't want to deal with it.

Even though I knew Patsy was right (and not just because she reminded me of that fact daily), I couldn't bring myself to call Mira and commit to attending Cassie's party. Whenever I reached for the phone, I froze. I was well aware how ridiculous I was being. It would take under three minutes to tell Mira I'd be there. It wouldn't even amount to a conversation, but still I hesitated.

Patsy had issued no fewer than five reminders to call Mira, and when she invited me to lunch at our favorite restaurant on Thursday, I knew I should have been suspicious of her motives. But the promise of a meal that didn't come from a can was too much to pass up. Almost as soon as the hostess seated us, Patsy (who always ordered either a cheeseburger or meatloaf and had no need to consult the menu) pointed out how rude I was being to my would-be hostess, as if I remained somehow unaware. She was unrelenting in her insistence that I commit to Cassie's party. I ignored her—or tried to—as I hid behind the menu deciding between chicken and pasta. The fact that Mira was on the receiving end of my bad manners did nothing to discourage Patsy's nagging. It also did nothing to make me feel better about throwing common courtesy overboard, especially when Patsy pointed out how unfair I was being to Cassie.

"She's expecting an answer, Liv."

"I know," I sighed, fiddling with my water glass and offering the least possible response to her habitual harassment. Acknowledging her opinion didn't slow her down at all.

"It's hardly fair to toy with a little girl's emotions like this, especially since she had no part in what happened to you."

"I know," I said again, feeling even worse about myself than before.

She wouldn't even let me back out after I told her that the party was in Highland Park—hardly a convenient location for a city girl without a car. Unless I wanted to spend half of my day on public transportation (I didn't) or ride my bike twenty miles each way, cultivating a force field of b.o. along the way, I had no way to get there.

"Take my car."

"Have you lost your mind?" She'd saved up for the better part of a year to buy her car, even though it would have been faster and easier to ask her dad to buy it for her. She cared for her car better than most people cared for their homes. "I can't do that."

"Sure you can. Just bring me a piece of cake and we'll call it even."

"Patsy, you love your car, and I don't drive."

"You know how, don't you?"

"In theory," I said, trying to remember the last time I'd been behind the wheel. I was pretty sure we'd had a different president.

"Just be careful. I trust you."

Though I found it odd that she was so invested in me attending Cassie's party, I quit arguing. I had no hope of winning when she was feeling determined.

"I'll bring you two pieces of cake."

"Deal," she said. Now all that was left was to call Mira when I got home.

I spent the rest of the afternoon giving myself intermittent pep talks whenever I thought of chatting with my enemy, and after a couple of false starts, I finally made the call. When Mira didn't immediately answer, I grew hopeful I'd get her voicemail, but she picked up right before my dreams came true. She sounded distracted, like I'd caught her in the middle of something (putting together a thirteen-year-old's birthday party maybe?), so I grew optimistic about my chances of making this a quick call.

"Mira, hi. It's Liv. Cucinelli. From the aquarium." I suppose I could have said from college, but if I had to have a relationship with her, no matter how fleeting and inconsequential, I'd prefer to assign it a more agreeable genesis than my former painful humiliation.

"Are you calling about the party? I hope you can make it. Cassie has been asking if you'll be coming, and I didn't know what to tell her."

No pressure, I thought, glad I wasn't calling to decline the invitation. "I'll be there," I told her.

"Wonderful!" Her enthusiasm was almost palpable. "I can't wait to share the good news with Cassie. She'll be so excited to see you. We both will, actually. We can spend some time catching up."

"Great," I replied, already wondering how I would evade Mira in her own home. "That sounds just great."

CHAPTER FOUR

I sat in Patsy's car for ten minutes, my heart filling with dread, my soul dying as I stared at the sprawling mansion Mira called home. The longer I sat there gaping at this monument to affluence and prosperity, the larger it became and the more out of place I knew I'd be. I just couldn't seem to make myself get out of the car and head into the party, even though I was already forty-five minutes late.

It wasn't that I was stalling. If anything, I wanted this over with, and I would have been on time, probably even early, if not for Patsy's GPS. It decided to take me on a tour of every wealthy neighborhood and suburb between her apartment and the party. It was like watching a parade of things I'd never be able to afford in this life or the next, culminating in the Midwest's answer to the Taj Mahal. If not for my strong desire to get out of the car I'd been trapped in for the last ninety minutes, I'm not sure anything would have motivated me to approach the palace looming before me and ring the bell.

It shouldn't have surprised me when a maid (in an honest-to-god maid uniform, frilly white apron and all) greeted me at the door, but I stood for another minute or two staring at this poor woman and wondering how the hell I was going to make it through the next few hours.   It felt like we stood in Mira's foyer for an hour. In actuality it was probably less than a minute, still more than enough time for me to feel even more out of place. The entryway to her palatial estate, with its polished marble floor and gleaming wood trim, was larger than my bedroom. I was pretty sure a troop of Girl Scouts could have held a meeting in her foyer with room left over for a pep rally.

Almost as soon as I left the privacy of the foyer and entered her living room, I knew coming to the party was a mistake. A quick glance around the room (chilly and not just from the air conditioning) told me I'd been a fool to think I wouldn't know anyone but Cassie and Mira. Of course the trio of backbiters who'd followed Mira's every move in college were sitting there, wearing the same fake smiles they'd have if their parents had photographed them on forced prom dates with their cousins. I don't know why I hadn't realized they'd be there (each one with a brood of genetically superior children in tow, no doubt). Mira had been their queen in college, and there was no reason to suspect things would be different now.

Still flustered from my drive and dreading the day's events, I walked into the Lion's Den—the opulent but impersonal living room where Mira's friends had gathered to criticize the poor and downtrodden, no doubt. The room—a veritable paean to beige and earth tones—lacked any warmth or human touches. Part of that was probably the dearth of children playing and having fun at what was supposed to be a child's birthday party, but the space also seemed like it was meant to be admired, not enjoyed. I got the impression that even the adults in the room were under harsh scrutiny and would be punished if anything was out of place when they left.

"Sorry I'm so late," I said, hating the good manners that forced me to apologize to Mira.

"Don't worry about it." She waved her hand in the air as if physically brushing aside my apology, making me feel oddly worse, like I owed her for excusing my lack of direction. "You remember Sarah, Megan and Tiffany." She breezed through the unnecessary introductions.

"How could I forget?" I said, sounding about as happy to see them as they appeared to be to see me. Ignoring the icy block of fear and dread settling in my stomach, I forced myself to smile instead of turning around and running back to the car.

For their part, they retained their unpleasantly surprised expressions and made no attempt at small talk. Either they'd been stunned into silence, or they were calculating the limits of outward rudeness they could show to their friend's guest. I was calculating how long they'd last before one of them brought up the past. On the plus side, none of them called me Ollie. Yet.

"Can I get you something to drink?"

"Please." I jumped at Mira's offer, though I held out little hope that alcohol would be available at a kid's party, not that I should indulge before my circuitous trek back to the city anyway.

Grateful for an escape, I followed her from the living room through the equally lavish dining room that could easily have held half my apartment. As we walked I mentally catalogued every item we passed that sat well outside my price range. Antique furniture. Boring but probably expensive artwork. Several pieces of ornate and delicate china. The pristine oak floors were adorned with gorgeous rugs, each of which looked like it would cost me a month's pay. I counted four on our walk from the living room to the kitchen.

I was way out of my league here. The only real exposure I'd ever had to wealth came from a handful of meals with Patsy's family, which was infinitely better off than mine. My mom raised me alone with zero help from my dad, who bailed the second the stick turned pink. But not even Patsy's family had money like this.

The part of my brain not calculating Mira's interior decorating allowance (and wondering what she did for a living that she could live so handsomely) was focused in part on the irony of Mira Butler being my savior. The thought that I might cling to her for the rest of the afternoon chilled me to the bone.

She chatted happily as we made our way from one end of her estate to the other. Apparently she hadn't been joking about wanting to catch up with me.

"How long have you been at the aquarium?"

"Twelve years." I sounded churlish to my own ears, and I knew I needed to shape up and act at least a little pleasant for Cassie's sake.

"You must like it," Mira said, unaffected by my terse response. "Five years is the longest I've managed to stay in any place, and I'm pushing that with my job now."

"What do you do?" I tried to deflect her interest and satisfy my curiosity at the same time.

"I'm the cosmetics manager at a department store."

Stunned, I took in my surroundings once more. While I wasn't surprised to learn she had a career dedicated to convincing women their natural beauty wasn't enough, there was no way a cosmetics manager could afford the home I was standing in. The idea that she'd married well occurred to me (not for the first time), but I couldn't figure out why a rich housewife would work at all, let alone shoot for the stars of cosmetics management.

"That sounds..." I struggled to find an inoffensive adjective.

"I think 'boring' is the word you're searching for."

"That's about right," I said. "Superficial" was really what I'd been thinking, but I didn't need to be rude.

"You don't really seem like the cosmetics type."

"Never have been."

She eyed me critically and smiled. "I don't think makeup would work for you."

"Was that supposed to be a compliment?"

She laughed and wrinkled her nose. "That didn't come out right. I meant you don't need any makeup. You look good without it."

Well, I certainly hadn't expected anything close to praise from her. This was turning out to be an interesting party after all.

"Are you married?" She resumed her interrogation, and as the questions grew more personal, I second-guessed my decision to follow her rather than take my chances in the living room.

"Not so far."

"Does that mean there's hope for the future?"

How big was this house anyway? For as far as we'd walked, we should have made it to the state line by now. "I'm about as much the marrying type as I am the cosmetics type."

"It's not for everyone," she said as we finally, blessedly crossed the threshold of her state-of-the-art kitchen. I got the impression the comment was more for her benefit than mine. I was pretty sure that if her marriage had been the source of her wealth, it wasn't the source of her happiness.

I was almost feeling bad for her and wondering what one says to one's downtrodden enemy when Cassie burst into the room, saving me from any sort of bonding or awkward attempt at comforting Mira. She was followed closely by a prim, pinched-faced woman with heavily sprayed hair and an outfit that suggested she had no concept of summer, children or birthday parties.

"Cassandra," the pursed woman barked, apparently unaware of Cassie's deafness. "Slow down. This isn't a gymnasium." She barely paused before turning her attentions on Cassie's mother. "Mira, the caterers are roaming around the yard aimlessly. Your party is going to be an embarrassing disaster if you leave them to their own devices, and I shudder at the thought of the broken English conversation with the landscapers to undo the mess these fools are sure to leave behind. Honestly, I don't know why you expect laypeople to show any initiative."

The part of me that wasn't perplexed by the idea of catering a thirteen-year-old's birthday party was desperately trying to avoid an encounter with this woman. I must have known we wouldn't both make it out alive.

"Excuse me, Liv," Mira said before turning to Satan's bride. "I'll take care of it, Mother." She asked Cassie to get me something to drink, and then she was gone, leaving me and Cassie alone with the living inspiration for class warfare.

Thankfully, I realized that in my commute-fueled frustration, I'd stupidly left Cassie's gift in the car. Though I hated to leave her alone with the least grandmotherly grandmother I'd ever encountered, I figured her lifetime of experience with Mrs.

Butler would offer her better coping mechanisms than the throat-punching method I favored.

Explaining my mistake to Cassie, I signed that I'd be right back. She looked resigned but not terrified. As I headed back the way I came, I felt Mrs. Butler's judgmental gaze on me. I fled the uncomfortable kitchen, sped through the acreage of Mira's home, past the gossiping gorgons and out to Patsy's car, the whole time marveling that Mira wasn't more unbearable, considering her lineage.

When I returned to the foyer with Cassie's gift in hand, I realized I'd become the topic of conversation. I didn't know if Mira's friends had mistaken my return to the car for an exit, or if they just didn't care that I might hear them, but I heard enough to know they were as petty and horrible as they'd been fifteen years earlier.

"I can't believe Mira let her come."

"She *invited* her."

"Isn't she worried Ollie will try something with Cassie?"

"If I had a daughter, I wouldn't let Ollie anywhere near her."

"What is Mira thinking?"

I couldn't tell whose voice was whose, but I was sure Sarah, Megan and Tiffany had all offered at least one unflattering remark. As I saw it, my options were to stand there listening to their hateful comments or to shut down the rumor mill and maybe make them feel bad, assuming they had the capacity to feel.

"You know, the one thing I was really liking about this little reunion was that no one had called me Ollie. Now you've gone and ruined that." They all threw on their best confused expressions, as if they had no idea what I was talking about. "It's weird, right? That I'm more upset over a silly nickname than the snide remarks, but honestly, I didn't expect anything else from the likes of you."

I left and headed for the relative sanctuary of the kitchen before they noticed I was so angry my hands were shaking.

Unfortunately, by the time I got back, that space was no less hostile than the one I'd just left.

Cassie had left the kitchen, whether by choice or at the command of her grandmother, I wasn't sure.

When Mrs. Butler saw me, she took one haughty glance at me, and based on her cold expression, she wasn't impressed.

"You used sign language with my granddaughter earlier."

She sounded both offended and accusatory, though I had no clue why she would be upset. I hadn't said anything inappropriate to Cassie in our thirty-second interaction. Since Mrs. Butler's tone made no sense, I pretended I hadn't picked up on it.

"I did," I answered more brightly than I'd spoken in the last decade. "It's been a few years since I've gotten to sign regularly. It's been fun to use it again."

"There's no need to coddle her."

"Excuse me? How is sign language coddling?"

"Cassie can read lips."

I rolled my eyes at her ridiculous assumption that lip reading in real life was anywhere close to being as miraculously accurate as it is in movies. How could someone be so willfully ignorant about her own family? How could she have such a narrow, hurtful worldview when it came to her granddaughter's well-being?

"If you use sign language, she'll be lazy about overcoming her...challenges."

Unbelievable. This woman seemed to equate Cassie's deafness with getting a cramp in a race, like Cassie could just tough it out or walk it off.

"You enable her disability by giving her the easy way out. She'll never be normal if she doesn't try, and she'll never try if she doesn't have to."

"Wait. You want your granddaughter to be normal when she's already exceptional? Why would you want her to be less than she is?"

Mrs. Butler glared at me. If I hadn't already suspected she and Beelzebub regularly conferred, I might have been taken aback by the look of pure hatred in her eyes. As it was, she just gave me more reason to despise her.

"My family, my rules," she said after a moment. "I'd suggest you abide by them if you intend to remain a part of my granddaughter's life."

"What about your daughter?"

"What about her?"

"Mira doesn't abide by *your* rules for *her* daughter. She uses sign language with Cassie, treats her with love and respect and doesn't think of her as an abnormality in need of changing. She actually allows Cassie to be herself and do what makes her comfortable." Now I'd defended Mira. Could this day get any weirder?

The cold expression Mrs. Butler had favored me with earlier was positively tropical compared to the look she gave me now.

"Maybe that's how your parents approached child-rearing, but allowing children to do whatever feels comfortable only encourages bad behavior…" Mira's mother paused in her invective long enough to look me up and down once more "… like giving in to one's more base impulses."

Given my vast experience with homophobia and the Butler family, it wasn't hard to know that her comment was directed at my lesbianism, though I'm not sure how she knew I was gay. True, I was the only female at the party in pants, and my short hair had no hope of being curled, braided, teased or styled in any manner that was close to girly, but it wasn't like I'd tattooed a rainbow on my forehead. Her comment showed a level of perception and ignorance I hadn't thought possible before I set foot in suburban Gehenna.

Rather than become embroiled in a debate with the incarnation of evil, I left the room without saying another word. It bothered me that she probably thought she'd won the argument and put me in my place, but I didn't have it in me then to champion gay rights, especially when I knew my points would go unheard or ignored. Already upset, hurt, enraged and far beyond my breaking point, I decided to leave before the day could get any worse. I doubted I'd be missed.

I didn't want to see Cassie when my anger was so close to the surface, but I wanted to make sure she got her present, which meant finding a gift table. Despite Mrs. Butler's lack of faith in the caterers, I figured they could point me in the right direction, so I headed the way Mira had gone earlier. She intercepted me at the edge of the enormous, lush, perfectly manicured lawn, and I thrust the gift into her hands.

"Please thank Cassie for the invitation."

"She's just over there if you want to thank her yourself."

"I'd rather just drop this off and go." I bit the words off.

"Liv, what's wrong?"

"I'm clearly not welcome, and I refuse to stay someplace where I'm insulted everywhere I go." She flinched, and her perfect brow furrowed. "I'm glad that I came, though. At least now I get it. I finally understand why you're such a horrible person. Who could grow up in the same house as that woman and turn out likeable? Just do the world a favor and don't pass the Butler family homophobia on to Cassie. She's a sweet kid and I'd hate to think she became a monster like you and your mother."

I could tell by her expression that I'd hit a nerve with that last comment, but I left her to her anger and her party. I was done.

CHAPTER FIVE

I made it two whole blocks before the tears started. I'm an angry crier, so the eventful half hour I'd just experienced pretty much secured my fate as a blubbering mess. I'd hoped I would get a little farther from Satan's palace before I blinded myself with my own rage, but I knew once the crying began, nothing but time (and possibly dehydration) would stop it.

Terrified I'd crash Patsy's car in my semi-blind state, I pulled over in front of yet another sprawling mansion. If not for the absence of any religious iconography, the place could easily have been mistaken for a cathedral—the Holy Temple of Luxury and Prosperity. I suspected the building's occupants were wondering what to do about the downtrodden mess outside their arched front doorway, assuming they could see beyond their upturned noses. If they had seen me and cared that I was there, I guessed they'd be more likely to have some private security force escort me from the premises than offer a sympathetic hug and some encouraging words. So, a little afraid of the further disaster the day could hold for me, I worked to calm myself down, and as soon as my tears subsided enough that I could talk, I called Patsy.

"Is the party over already?"

"It is for me," I answered, my voice still shaky.

"What on earth did they do to you?" She sounded both supportive and protective, like she was ready to hug me and beat up the bad guys simultaneously.

I spilled the whole story from the crazy GPS adventure to Mrs. Butler's venom spewing in the kitchen. She tsked and groaned conspiratorially as I filled her in on all the details, and she didn't even point out that I had been somewhat unfair to Mira for unleashing on her what I should have directed at her mother.

"Who knew Mira was the gem of the family?" was her only comment.

"I'm still holding out hope for Cassie—if she runs away. But why did I think I could spend time with her mother? She's just as evil as ever. No kid is worth that."

"Don't hate me for asking, but what did Mira do?"

"What do you mean?" Had Patsy not heard anything I just said?

"I would classify Mira's behavior, at least what you've described so far, as courteous and polite, maybe bordering on friendly. So was there something else? Did she hurt you too? Or are you just calling her evil because that's historically accurate?"

I flashed back on the events of the afternoon and realized that Patsy was right. Rather than abusing me with the rest of the coven of cruelty, Mira had been nothing but kind. I stayed silent so long replaying the party, trying to find some fault with her behavior and grappling with Patsy's bizarre suggestion that Mira might not be entirely malevolent, she must have realized it could take me decades to acknowledge any positive attribute in Mira. She gave up waiting for an answer.

"I'm sorry I made you go. I had no idea it would be that bad."

"I wish it had only been *that bad*. Compared to what I just went through, *that bad* would have been a piece of cake. Oh crap!"

"What now?"

"I never got your birthday cake."

"Go back."

"No way!" I was pretty sure she wasn't serious, but she loved sweets, and I wasn't about to hedge my bets.

"You should be compensated for your ordeal. Demand restitution in the form of dessert. You're entitled to baked goods for life after what they've put you through."

I should have known she would find a way to make me laugh. Even at the worst points of my life, she'd always gotten at least a smile out of me. Usually she had me giggling at inappropriate moments—like my mother's wake. Even though I didn't appreciate the curious and judgmental looks thrown my way by other mourners, I was better for not wallowing in my misery.

I don't know why Patsy had chosen me as a friend, but I knew I was lucky to have her, so I decided I had to do something to show my appreciation. Maybe, if I could get the GPS to cooperate, I'd find a bakery between her house and the side street I had just bathed in my tears. I was contemplating cookies and cupcakes with flowers and sprinkles, all the treats she liked best, when she interrupted my thoughts.

"Can you handle driving yet, or do I need to send out the cavalry?"

"I'm much better now. Thanks."

"I live to serve."

"I'll see you soon, assuming your GPS doesn't send me to Indiana first."

"Just get here in one piece and I'll have a drink waiting for you."

Knowing her, that drink would turn into a trip to the bar, a trip I looked forward to, even though I had to work the next day.

Two days later I'd mostly gotten past my anger. It helped to think that, unless the fates conspired against me, I'd never have to see or speak to Mira Butler again. That idea alone was almost euphoric. On top of that, I spent my lunchbreak on Sunday in the sea otter nursery, where the aquarium's newest addition, an orphaned and as yet nameless pup was learning important otter life skills like grooming and opening his own shellfish.

One of the benefits of working as an aquarist is the peace and calm I get just by being near the animals I care for. I haven't conducted a study to verify my hypothesis, but I'm reasonably sure there isn't a problem on earth than can't be made better by watching sea otters for ten or fifteen minutes. So thanks to the pup (as well as the fishes and other creatures I spent my time with) my workday on Sunday had been almost like a therapy session. I went home much happier than I'd been when I started my day, and by lunch on Monday I was on the verge of giddy thanks to a mid-morning meeting with my boss.

Not long after my morning rounds, he called me into his office for a little chat. I was somewhat concerned that he wanted to talk about my lack of fundraising ideas, but he had a different, more pleasant matter in mind.

"We haven't had an opportunity to discuss your most recent class, and I wanted to touch base with you about it."

I had been anxiously wondering when I would hear the feedback. Even though I felt good about the class after it ended, it killed me not knowing if it had been deemed successful enough to run again next summer.

"The response has been overwhelmingly positive. So much so that the board would like to implement a follow-up course in a few weeks. I know that's not much time to plan, but we want to get it on the schedule before school starts up again. I hope you're up for it."

Even if I'd wanted to, I couldn't have stopped the smile that spread across my face.

"The students and their parents enjoyed the work you did, and I'd like to have you on board for this."

"Absolutely. I already have some ideas," I answered without hesitating. Did he think I'd want someone else taking over with my girls? No way.

For almost half an hour, we discussed scheduling and my thoughts for the direction of the course, and I left his office excited about the class and welcoming my former students back to a more in-depth study of specific animals than the overview they'd already enjoyed. I couldn't wait to see which of them would return. I hoped Cassie would be among the repeat pupils, even though that meant confronting Mira, who I was more than happy to ignore.

Soon after that conversation, though, my mood plummeted, thanks to an unexpected call from her. I answered the phone, anticipating the usual update or question from my colleagues— about the training schedule for our giant Pacific octopuses, our coral breeding, or any of the other issues that popped up during the course of pretty much every day at the aquarium. What I got instead was an ambush from the woman I was trying to forget about. She didn't sound nearly as bright as the last time we'd spoken on the phone, but that was small comfort.

"Liv? It's Mira. I'm sorry to bother you, but Cassie needs to know where to send a thank you for the gift. She loves it, by the way."

"I'm glad," I said. "She doesn't need to send a thank you."

"Yes, she does."

"Send it to the aquarium, I guess."

"Oh, okay. We will."

"Was there something else?" I asked after a lengthy pause.

"Yes, actually." She cleared her throat, and again I felt a little satisfied by her discomfort. "I also want to apologize, but we're both at work. It's hardly ideal for the conversation we need to have. There's not enough time, and I'd like to say what I have to say in person."

"There's nothing I want to hear from you or say to you. Wait, that's not actually true. There's plenty I want to say to you. I just don't think it will make any difference."

"I know you're angry, furious probably, and I don't blame you. But I promise if you give me the chance to apologize and explain, I won't ask you for anything else. I'll leave you alone."

"Why can't you just leave me alone now?"

"Not until you hear me out. After I say what I need to say, I won't bother you again."

"Why does it matter so much?"

"I'm not the person you think I am, Liv. I think you should at least know the full story. If you decide you still want to hate me after you hear everything, well, at least you'll be making an informed decision, which seems like a more logical approach than being ruled by your emotional response to things."

"I'm not Spock," I retorted, though I realized she had a point.

"I know," she said. It sounded like she might have been trying not to laugh. "But don't scientists usually try to gain a fuller understanding of things? I mean, it's not very reasonable to learn half the story and accept that as the truth, is it?"

Damn. She had me there. I wondered if Cassie had coached her. I didn't want to let her off easy, though.

"Are you going to keep harassing me until I hear you out?"

"Pretty much." She laughed a little uncomfortably, which I enjoyed. At least this wasn't easy for her. "Cassie would love to see you. She was upset that she didn't really get to say goodbye at the party."

I groaned in irritation and dragged out an irritated sigh. As angry as I was with her, I hated that Cassie had gotten caught up in all of our adult drama. I didn't want to give in, but . . .

"I'll make you dinner."

I stayed silent, still weighing my options.

"Please Liv, let me at least try to make this right."

I'm not sure what it was, but something in her voice wore me down. "Fine. Let's get this over with. When and where?"

"Thursday is my next free evening. Does that work for you?"

"Sure," I said, about as enthusiastic as a patient waiting for a rectal exam. "Where?"

"Why don't you come to my house?"

"I don't have a way to get back out to Highland Park. I borrowed Patsy's car for the birthday party." Maybe I could get out of this after all. I silently cheered my transportation obstacles.

"The party was at my mother's house. I live in Lincoln Square, just off the Brown Line, so you don't need a car."

Damn.

CHAPTER SIX

I spent far too much time over the next three days pondering what excuses Mira would likely offer up to explain her and her mother's homophobic behavior. I didn't come up with anything remotely believable (Nutritional deficiency? Tiny suburban cult? Alien abduction and subsequent brainwashing?), but it was a great distraction. Excursions into fantasy aside, I was nervous about my appointment with the devil. I doubted she could produce any acceptable explanation for her behavior toward me, but what if she did? Would that mean I would have to forgive her? Was that even something I wanted to do? I didn't know, and the closer I got to Thursday night's dinner, the more anxious I became.

By the time I finally showed up for our skirmish, I had built the whole thing up in my mind so much that I was a little disappointed when I arrived at Mira's house. For one thing, it was just a normal house—a brick bungalow that, though it was still about a thousand times larger than my apartment, was at least ten times smaller than Mrs. Butler's palatial estate in Highland

Park. I hated to admit it, but Mira's house was adorable. There were no outward indications that evil incarnate dwelled within those innocuous brick walls. None of her neighbors appeared to be wary of her, the air didn't reek of sulfur, and the green grass of her lawn showed no signs of the scorched earth that should have surrounded her lair. By all appearances, it was a normal, unassuming, non-demonic house, which chilled me to the bone.

The interior was even worse. The space was tidy, well decorated and homey. Unlike her mother, Mira incorporated bright colors. I didn't conduct a thorough search, but my cursory glances around the open, inviting space of her living and dining room revealed not an ounce of beige or a hint of earth tones. The walls were a sort of turquoise, and splashes of orange in the rug and on the furniture reminded me of the coral reef exhibit at the aquarium. There was warmth and personality in this space. It was a home, not just a house, and that surprised me.

Mira and I stood awkwardly for several minutes, neither of us knowing what to say. Emotionally speaking, I would have preferred if she would just blurt out her apology and whatever excuse she'd managed to dream up so that I could leave, but my stomach had other ideas. Based on the mouth-watering aromas wafting from the kitchen, either she'd hired a professional chef or knew how to cook, which is more than could ever be said about me. A meal that didn't come from a box, bag or can was a rare treat for me. Most of the so-called food in my kitchen was processed garbage with a shelf life a tortoise would envy. None of it had any right to be called food, but it was quick and easy, and it kept me from starving to death.

I stubbornly refused to tell her whatever she was cooking smelled divine (or to say anything to her if I didn't have to). She was equally tongue-tied, whether from nerves or guilt, I wasn't sure. The quiet in the room grew almost unbearable, enveloping us in awkward, stony silence, broken only by Cassie's blessed appearance on the scene, first to hug and then to chastise me.

"You left my birthday party without saying goodbye." She put her hands on her hips and stuck her chin out, obviously demanding an apology and an explanation for my rudeness. Stuck in that awkward space between childhood and womanhood, she was adorable and a little bit intimidating. I felt horrible for letting her down.

"I'm sorry I had to leave, Cassie, but I suddenly didn't feel well and couldn't stay." It was more or less the truth, and my lie of omission might spare Cassie from realizing her ties to the minions of hell.

Cassie nodded slowly, as if mulling over my excuse. Then she asked if I'd read the latest issue of *Scientific American* and what I thought of the article on desalination. In no time, I was absorbed in a discussion of sustainability and global conservation efforts with one of the brightest young minds I had ever encountered.

Meanwhile, Mira had left the room, which I only realized when she returned and handed me a beer (which I eagerly accepted) before telling us that dinner was ready.

At the dinner table, I kept my focus on Cassie, asking about her summer and what classes she was most excited about when school started in a few weeks. Even though Mira interjected regularly, my chat with Cassie allowed me to ignore Mira for the most part and helped me prolong dinner, which I suspected was the only thing standing between me and some uncomfortable one-on-one time with her. Even though none of the details had been finalized, I also told Cassie about the new class at the aquarium, causing her to jump from her seat in excitement. Mira seemed equally pleased.

"How about it, Cassie? Are you interested?"

For an answer, Cassie hugged her mom and then me. Her radiant smile never left her face. Even if nothing else good came from this night, her joy in that moment made my otherwise ever-present discomfort completely worthwhile.

"Cassie hasn't talked about anything else since the last class ended. She's obsessed with fish now. I hope you're happy."

"I am," I answered, my cool demeanor standing in stark contrast to what I felt in that moment.

I could tell my terse response bothered Mira. Her habitual smiles never reached her eyes, and she kept fidgeting with her silverware, but she never quit trying to interact. Her tenacity was surprising and impressive, and I started to feel a little guilty for giving her such a hard time. I was a guest in her home, invited over to hear her out and get a long overdue apology. I decided to be more gracious to my host. Or at least less hostile. I didn't get much of an opportunity to act on my resolution before our meal ended and Mira sent Cassie off to her best friend's house.

"What about the dishes?" Cassie asked, her face a lovely blend of eagerness and trepidation.

"I've got another helper tonight," Mira told her, and after a quick but enthusiastic hug for each of us, Cassie was out the door.

"She's a good kid," I said as I started stacking plates to clear the table.

"She is. I'm lucky." She laid her hand on my arm. "You don't really have to help with the dishes. I just didn't want Cassie to be around for this."

"The big apology." I sighed and sank back into my seat. I'd been imagining this moment for years, but now that it had arrived, I felt nauseous and terrified.

Mira didn't speak for a while. Instead she cleared her throat, wrung her hands and stared at the floor. I started to think she would never get on with it. I even contemplated how to get her started, but eventually she cleared her throat again and found her voice.

"It's probably lame just to say I'm sorry, but I am."

"For which of your many offenses are you apologizing, Mira?"

"All of them, I guess."

"Come on. You're going to have to do better than that." No way was I letting her off with such a vague, noncommittal apology.

"This isn't easy for me," she said, and I could hear in her voice how difficult she found it, but I found that even more infuriating than her previous silence. Why should she feel put out or allowed to play the victim over belated remorse?

"Should it be? It's not like my life was a breeze after you told everyone I raped you."

"I didn't. That's not what I said."

I glared at her. She opened her mouth to speak and then stopped, apparently thinking better of it. Whatever she was about to tell me was obviously not as defensible as she'd hoped. Taking advantage of her vulnerability, I lashed out at her then. "Tell me, Mira. What innocent comment of yours got twisted into a vicious rumor that forced me to leave the dorms, necessitated a job I had no time for, lost me my scholarship and put me a year behind in school?"

"I started showering on a different floor, and when Tiffany asked why, I said it was because of you, because I thought you…" she looked away, shame and guilt clouding her expression.

"Because you thought what? That I was likely to violate another human being in maybe the most heinous, horrible way possible?"

"No, Liv. I never said that, I swear. I don't know who started that rumor, but it wasn't me."

"Then what did you say?" She looked like she just swallowed a porcupine, but I refused to let her squirm her way out of acknowledging just how much she'd hurt me. "Tell me, Mira."

"I said I thought you were creepy and gross, and I was afraid to be around you."

"That's so much better. I don't know why I've been so upset all these years."

"I know what I said was terrible, but it was just an innocent comment to my friend."

"Innocent? People copied everything you did, Mira. Even if you didn't start the rumor, you contributed to it. Your so-called innocent comment was enough to make me a pariah, and if that had been the worst that happened, I could have lived with it. But it wasn't. My god! Do you have any idea what you did to me?"

"I just assumed after you left the dorm—"

"I left school, Mira, not just the dorms. I had to get a job to pay for a crappy apartment that wasn't worth half of what I paid in rent, but I had no time to work. I was taking eighteen credit hours a semester. I couldn't keep up. My grades slipped—just in a couple of courses, but it was enough. I lost my scholarship."

Mira looked horrified, and though I always thought it would be satisfying to see the consequences of her actions etched on her beautiful face, it failed to live up to my expectations. It was almost difficult to witness her anguish over the damage she'd caused, but I pressed on anyway.

"Without a scholarship, I couldn't stay in school, and without school, there was no reason to stay in Charleston. So I bailed. I ran to my mother, but when I got home, she was different. She'd lost weight. She looked awful. I thought she was just worried about me, but—"

"Oh, no," Mira gasped, and her hand covered her mouth.

"By the time she went to the doctor, it was too late. Stage four ovarian cancer. She only lasted a few months."

"Oh, Liv, I'm so sorry."

"It gave me an easy excuse when I came back to school in the fall. I didn't risk the dorms again, but if anyone asked where I'd been—and a few people did—I could be the girl who left to take care of her dying mother instead of the emotionally unstable gay girl. I mean, if you could choose, who would you rather be?"

I felt oddly relieved to have unleashed all of that on Mira, like she might—finally—understand how selfish and cruel she'd been. But there was no satisfaction in seeing the tears in her eyes as I scowled at her.

"I can't even begin to imagine how you must have felt, or to express to you just how sorry I am about what happened." She spoke softly, her voice unsteady, but her eyes never left mine. "Believe me, If I had known then what I know now, I wouldn't have been so stupid. But I was young and naïve. I believed what my mother told me about gay people, and I'd never met a…a lesbian before. I didn't have any evidence to the contrary." I met her words with angry silence. "I'm sorry about what I did and how it affected you. If I'd known what people were saying about you at the time, I would have put a stop to it."

"Of course," I spoke bitterly. "I'm sure you would have gone out of your way to defend the creepy lesbian you were trying to avoid."

"I was a fool, Liv, not a liar," she snapped in a quick burst of anger. "I'm willing to contact every girl from our residence hall to set the record straight. I already started on Saturday with Megan, Sarah and Tiffany."

"Why? Most of the girls who lived there have probably forgotten about it. It doesn't even matter now."

"It's as close as I can get to undoing it, and it does matter. It obviously still hurts you, and if this is going to keep you away from Cassie, I need to try to fix it."

"Don't drag up the past. I've lived with this hanging over me for so long I'm used to it. Just let it go, please." I felt exhausted. All I wanted was to go to sleep so I could forget this entire day.

"You haven't accepted my apology yet. I can't let it go."

"Why? Why can't you just leave me alone?"

"Because…a lifetime ago, without even knowing it, I did the worst thing I've ever done. Now all I can do is offer an apology and hope you can forgive me. God!" She started pacing as she spoke, her words tumbling out in a rush. "I brought you so much misery and gave you every reason to despise me when, if I hadn't been so cruel and stupid, we probably would have been friends. I think I would've loved being your friend, but I ruined that chance. Now I can't even hope you'll like me."

"I've hated you for almost twenty years. I'm not sure I'm ready to start liking you."

"Can you at least try to stop hating me?"

Since Mira had reentered my life, my only thoughts of her had been about how much I hated her. The idea of just not hating her had never occurred to me. It was so simple. I wasn't sure I could manage it.

"I'm not a bad person, Liv. I made a mistake when I was young and too stupid to know better. I know better now."

Looking at Mira—her hands shaking, her face a teary mess—I had no doubt that her apology had been sincere. I almost felt bad for how bad she felt, not bad enough to be her new best friend, but certainly enough to let her off the hook.

"Thank you for apologizing, Mira. I appreciate it." I couldn't bring myself to say, "I forgive you," not because I didn't, but because I thought it would make me sound like a priest or a judge absolving her of her past crimes. Only she could do that.

Before I knew what was happening, she hugged me. Initially I froze (up to that point, I'd hugged all of four people in my life), but eventually I returned the embrace. It was strange, holding a woman whom I'd previously only dreamed of throttling. I again considered Mira's suggestion that I stop hating her.

I didn't know where Mira and I stood at that moment or how to define our strange new relationship, and while I was still angry about the past, I thought, maybe, given enough time, I might leave my anger and my hatred for Mira behind me.

CHAPTER SEVEN

"So she *accidentally* called you a rapist? *That's* her excuse?"

Incredulous, Patsy stomped to her kitchen for more beer. She'd drained hers while I shared the evening's developments, but I'd been so busy talking that I'd hardly touched the drink she brought me half an hour earlier.

"According to her, she didn't call me a rapist at all. That was someone who heard her creepy and gross comment and decided to raise the bar on defamation."

After Mira's apology, I'd stopped by Patsy's apartment unannounced, seeking counsel but was beginning to doubt the wisdom of looking to Patsy for clarity. Not only were our feelings on the subject too closely aligned, but Patsy also seemed especially far removed from clarity that evening. Based on the skunky aroma lingering in the air, I guessed that her plans hadn't included me and my discomposure setting up camp in her living room (though she really should have been expecting us). I'd probably interrupted some quality slothful downtime for Patsy, and despite her casual welcome, I felt bad for intruding on her evening, relaxed though it was.

"And you believe her?" She dropped herself onto the couch next to me and fixed me with an unwavering, glassy-eyed stare.

Not for the first time since leaving her home, I mulled over what Mira told me earlier. I supposed she could have lied to me about college, but that didn't add up. Rather than admitting the horrible things she said, she could just as easily have denied talking about me at all. Since I had only lived through the aftermath of her words rather than hearing them firsthand, I had no way of proving she'd ever spoken about me, so denial was a plausible tactic.

And up until I snapped at Cassie's birthday party, Mira had seemed oblivious to my feelings about her. She wasn't stupid, so if she had told the world I raped her, there was no way she wouldn't know that I hated her. On top of that, her distress during her apology had seemed genuine. Either her confession had been the truth, or she had a solid future in the theater.

"Yeah, I do."

"Okay." Patsy drew the word out to about four syllables, her disdain evident. "So now what? Did you kiss and make up? Are you friends now? Oh god," she gasped. "Do I have to be her friend too?"

"Relax, drama queen. I haven't even forgiven her yet. I just accepted her apology and left."

"Without getting dessert. Again." Patsy rose abruptly and headed back into the kitchen.

"How thoughtless of me not to interrupt Mira's heartfelt apology to request some pie." My eye roll was lost on Patsy as she foraged through her cabinets. I debated following her on her quest for a satisfying stand-in for pie, but she returned shortly with a box of S'mores Pop-Tarts and handed me a sleeve.

"Do you think you will?" I must have looked as baffled as I felt because she added, "Forgive her. You said you didn't forgive her yet."

"I don't know," I muttered around a mouthful of sugary goodness. "I'm still trying to understand how this all happened. Essentially, my life got upended and made hell in college because of a colossal misunderstanding. That's a little hard to make peace with."

"You really think there would have been no turmoil if not for Mira saying something stupid that turned into something terrible?" Patsy's skepticism was palpable.

"Up until then no one seemed to care."

"No one knew. You were selectively out."

"Which was obviously a wise choice," I snapped. As one of half a dozen people in college who knew about my sexuality before the scandal, Patsy was right, but I was still reeling from Mira's bombshell, and I wasn't interested in reexamining younger me's choice to stay closeted, especially since, had I stuck with that plan, I never would have had to deal with the harsh consequences of Mira's youthful ignorance. "I'm not saying the other girls would have hit the gay bars with me or tried to set me up with their friends from the soccer team. Some of them probably would have avoided me. A few might even have made nasty comments about me, but I could have ignored the general discomfort my sexuality *might* have caused a hell of a lot easier than dodging the hostility, panic and repulsion that my alleged assault *did* cause."

"I suppose," she sighed her grudging agreement.

"I'm sure anyone who cared about my sexuality would have preferred a lesbian in the dorm over a rapist. Faced with a similar situation, I'd much rather share space with a homophobe than a rapist. You know the rape comment is what made the situation unbearable."

"And that's exactly why you shouldn't be so quick to brush it aside and forgive her."

"I'm not brushing anything aside. I just think it's maybe more understandable now." She glared at me. "It was still an asshole move, just not as asshole as I've been thinking all these years."

I considered how much time and energy I'd squandered in almost twenty years over something that hadn't really happened, at least not the way I'd believed. What a waste. No doubt I would have been hurt and angry to know what Mira really had said about me, but I could have chalked it up to small-minded bigotry, cut ties and moved on. I wouldn't have spent almost half my life stewing about it.

"You're being awfully understanding and mature about this while I'm wondering how she'd react to me *accidentally* driving a flaming sword through her chest."

"As long as you apologized afterward, I'm sure she'd understand," I said, shaking my head as my pothead avenging angel struggled with the cellophane barrier between her and her second sleeve of Pop-Tarts.

In the brief time between Mira's sincere but less than satisfying apology and the class that would bring Cassie back into my life, time either passed at warp speed or moved in reverse. There was no happy medium. Though I knew this wasn't a phenomenon particular to me, my case seemed peculiar in that my workdays flew by while my leisure time stretched out interminably. Hours passed like decades and weekends became millennia—a blessing for most of the work-weary labor force, but a curse for me as I scrambled for ways to avoid thinking about Mira Butler and her apology.

Nothing I distracted myself with preoccupied me for long, and after three weeks I still hadn't figured out if I could stop hating her or even forgive her. Obviously I needed to come to some kind of resolution soon. I counted on seeing Cassie in my class, and though that didn't guarantee Mira and I would cross paths, I knew better than to hope I could avoid seeing her again. I didn't believe in fate, but lately it seemed like something out there was determined to bring us together. When that happened, it wouldn't do for me to stumble around in an emotional morass.

Nevertheless, my primary strategy was still to avoid dealing with the situation, a proven method for past emotional quandaries. So I worked as much as my boss allowed, and outside of work I rode my bike, watched old movies or pestered Patsy, a course of action that ended up being less helpful than I'd hoped.

After the night of Mira's apology, Patsy refused to let me off the hook. Even when our conversation could in no way be connected to Mira, Patsy always brought it around to that sore subject by asking if I'd made up my mind yet. I knew she had my best interests at heart, but soon I started avoiding her as well, leaving me with no choice but to troll the bars in search of strangers who neither knew nor cared about my Mira dilemma. That's how I met Tara.

In town for a few days and in search of a good time with no commitment (in other words, my perfect woman), Tara proved to be more than just a pleasant physical distraction. When our minimal conversation rolled around to my job, she shrieked, startling me. After telling me that she visited the aquarium whenever she came to Chicago and asking (in a manner that made saying no almost impossible) if she could get a private tour, Tara asked about the aquarium's newest and most popular resident.

"Do you get to play with the baby otter?" Her voice conveyed a childlike enthusiasm in direct opposition to the completely adult, tousled hair, total lack of modesty scene spread across her hotel bed.

"I visit him regularly," I said, not wanting to dash her hopes with the potentially disappointing news that I spent my days tending to fishes from Asia and Africa rather than "playing" with cuddly marine mammals.

"I would never get any work done if he was at my job. I would just stare at him all day. He's such a cutie."

"He's adorable," I agreed. "But I think all of our animals are beautiful, not just Eight-twenty-four."

"Eight-twenty-four? That's what you call him?" She sounded shocked that we hadn't given the pup a proper name yet, but we were more concerned about getting him back to health and helping him learn how to be an otter. And though we would never admit it, our science backgrounds didn't prevent us from falling victim to certain superstitions, which meant none of us wanted to jinx him with a name before he started to thrive.

"That's the number he was assigned by the facility that rescued him. Once he's stable in his new home, we'll worry about a name."

"Poor baby. He needs a name, not a number." She propped herself up on her elbows and looked down at me. "You should let me name him, especially since you're all so busy."

"What would you call him?" I asked.

I don't know if she'd been pondering the possibilities for a while or if she was just adept at naming otters, but she rattled off an impressive list of monikers, including Harry Otter, Colonel Sherman T. Otter and Barnaby.

The rest slipped my attention. Though I was curious to know what Tara considered an appropriate name for a sea otter pup, my thoughts drifted off in the direction of a fundraising idea that she had inadvertently planted. It was an idea so simple and obvious I couldn't believe no one had suggested it yet, and as she rambled on about otter names, I formulated the skeleton of a proposal centered on letting the public suggest and vote on names for Pup 824. I knew my boss could figure out some way to monetize the idea, and if I suggested it, I wouldn't have to dodge his subtle, daily admonishments about the fundraising campaign. Tara was turning out to be one of the most beneficial flings I'd ever had, and I was almost sad when we parted ways early Sunday morning.

CHAPTER EIGHT

Roman loved my fundraising idea and launched the Name the Otter campaign as quickly as possible—on the last day of my follow-up class with the girls, as it turned out. He'd handed my suggestion over to the aquarium's tiny marketing team, and they had transformed it into an all-out fundraising offensive. So it happened that, upon arrival for the start of class that day, each of my students passed under a banner announcing her opportunity to help decide Pup 824's name. Considering they had also undoubtedly encountered numerous billboards and buses promoting the public's chance to help our otter pup escape his nameless plight, I guessed I'd have a hard time keeping their focus. I didn't mind, though, since, in a way, I was also the source of their distraction. It was a great start to my day.

Earlier in the week I'd taken the girls on a behind the scenes tour to refresh their memories and reignite their interest in what we'd be doing the rest of the week. I'd made a point of visiting with the team caring for Pup 824, affording the girls a glimpse of the aquarium's unwitting savior as he worked to groom himself. If their collective "Aww" was any indication, they fell in love with him immediately, so it didn't surprise me that, on the last day of class, they asked me a thousand questions about the Name the Otter campaign.

Later, on a small break, I allowed my inner busybody to eavesdrop as the girls shared their ideas on what to call the aquarium's superstar. Even Cassie, who usually kept to herself when I wasn't around to sign and interpret for her, offered a few suggestions, writing them down and passing them around. Based on the other girls' reactions, Cassie's ideas were good ones, but I was left in the dark as they passed papers back and forth within the group and giggled.

Watching them there, gathered for a course I'd invented, eager to participate in a contest I'd dreamed up, I felt proud of myself and my accomplishments—everything about the class had gone well, so well that my mood bordered on euphoria. That feeling remained more or less in place until the end of the day.

Up to that point, I'd successfully avoided the Mira question simply by avoiding Mira. As luck would have it, on the days when Cassie left with her mother instead of her grandmother, I was busy talking to other parents, allowing me to send Cassie off with a wave or nod, some sort of nonverbal acknowledgement that I was passing her off to safe hands. Twice, Cassie's grandmother had picked her up, and on the days when Cassie trudged away with the North Shore's own Darth Vader in a pantsuit, our mutual distaste kept us apart, like the repellent properties of like magnetic poles. It worked out perfectly.

On Friday, however, long after the other students departed, Cassie lingered in the vicinity of the aquarium gift shop, eyeing a stuffed blue-spotted stingray with that peculiar blend of childish longing and mature disdain for the relics of childhood that was singular to adolescent girls. Class had ended only twenty minutes earlier, so I didn't think all-out panic was warranted just yet, but I was somewhat apprehensive. Up to that point, Cassie had never been among the stragglers left waiting for a tardy parent or nanny to escort them home. It seemed odd that no one had come to claim her yet, but it was still early enough to fall into the window of excusable tardiness.

I couldn't leave her alone in the lobby (and not just because my position required me to ensure the safety of all of my students from arrival to departure), so concerned for Cassie and cautiously optimistic about putting an end to my day, I interrupted her conflicted window shopping to ask if everything was all right.

"Mom's late."

"Mind if I wait with you?" I asked, guessing that Cassie would be more receptive to adult supervision if she thought she had a choice in the matter. She smiled and nodded her agreement before we wandered away from the enticing gift shop.

Thinking Mira must be stuck in rush hour traffic (doubly horrendous on a Friday in the summer), and hoping she would show up soon, I opted not to call her for the time being. If she was driving, she couldn't (or shouldn't) talk, and I didn't want to make her worry. Cassie would be fine with me for the time being.

Instead, I tried to distract her (and myself) from the minutes ticking by with no sign of Mira. We milled about the lobby as Cassie peppered me with questions about my education and what I thought were the best schools for aspiring chemists, physicists or marine biologists (a line of questioning I was only partially up to the task of addressing).

Meanwhile I kept an eye on the doors and grew increasingly annoyed every time someone who wasn't Mira passed through them. Though I knew she loved Cassie and I doubted she would forget or neglect her child, Mira was now over forty-five minutes late and, as far as I knew, had made no attempt to reassure her daughter or her daughter's temporary guardian that we hadn't slipped her mind.

Cassie seemed remarkably calm considering that her mother, close to an hour late, was MIA, so I tried to convey the same serenity. Underneath the surface, though, I was fuming. It was so irresponsible and inconsiderate of Mira to keep us waiting without word of when she thought she might arrive. If she'd been present as my mind was silently cataloguing every instance of her supreme selfishness, I probably would have gotten myself in trouble for forgetting to be polite to the paying public. So when she finally appeared, I found it almost impossible to remain civil.

"I'm so sorry I'm late." She took a moment to study her daughter's face before pulling her in for a hug. "Thank you so much, Liv, for staying with Cassie until I got here," she said. Then, still holding Cassie to her, she apologized again. My anger flared.

"It was no problem really," I said, unable to keep the acerbic tone from my voice. "It's not like I had anything better to do, and I'm sure you had some mascara emergency to deal with." Mira, still clinging to her daughter, flinched. Feeling an odd satisfaction at her reaction, I barreled ahead. "But now that the women of Chicago are properly equipped to paint their faces, I'd like to get back to my day."

She blinked several times, tears glistening in her eyes and threatening to fall any second. Worse, now that I really looked at her, I could tell these weren't the first tears she'd shed that day. Though she'd obviously tried to hide it, the telltale red and puffy eyes that not even a cosmetics professional like herself could cover up gave her away. If I had taken even half a second to look at her before opening my big mouth, I would have noticed her obvious distress.

I didn't think I'd been that harsh (and really, she worked with the public on a regular basis, so she should have developed better coping skills than this), but standing there, watching her try not to cry in front of her kid and losing that battle, I felt bad for her. I got the strong sense that something terrible had happened, something she was trying to keep from Cassie. Even having no clue what had upset her or why she'd been delayed didn't prevent me from feeling partly responsible for her current struggle for composure.

"Of course," Mira said, her voice noticeably shaky. "Thank you again. I'm sorry to have bothered you." She released Cassie from her marathon embrace and laid a trembling hand on her daughter's shoulder.

Still clinging to Cassie, Mira turned to leave, and as they walked away, Cassie threw a supportive arm around her mother. I watched them making their slow way across the aquarium's rapidly emptying lobby, and I thought about Cassie trying to be an adult and care for her mother while Mira's motherly instincts refused to allow it. Undoubtedly she would want to keep Cassie a child, safe from whatever ugliness the world had shown her that day. The whole situation seemed impossibly sad.

"Oh what the hell," I muttered, astounded at what I was about to do. "Mira, wait," I called out and struggled to reach them in the throng of visitors pouring out of the aquarium.

Mira turned to look at me, and I could tell she was no better off than when we'd parted a moment before. In fact, her chin had started quivering in her attempt to hold back her tears. Almost her entire red, blotchy face had joined in on the effort, but anger flashed in her eyes. I got the impression that she was in no mood to deal with me, and that, had she trusted her voice at that moment, she would have pointed out that I'd said enough.

I floundered a bit in the face of her wrath. Angry as she was, she didn't seem likely to take me up on the offer I was about to make. Still, I thought they both could benefit from Mira having some support other than her teenage daughter, so I did what any rational adult would—I resorted to subterfuge.

"How about some ice cream?" I asked, directing my offer to Cassie, who responded exactly as I'd hoped she would. Her eyes widened before I'd even finished the sign for "ice cream," and she immediately turned to her mother to beg permission for a summer treat.

Mira glared at me, and I shrank a little in the face of her seething hostility. Cassie noticed the shift in her mother as well, and the eager bouncing that had started at the mention of ice cream stopped abruptly. On the plus side, Mira's anger made her tears subside, but at the moment that seemed to be the only positive result of my action.

Again communicating directly with Cassie, I asked her to give me some time to convince her mother. "Go look at the stuffed animals in the gift shop, and I'll be there in five minutes,"

I signed. "Better make it ten," I amended after a withering glance from Mira.

"I thought you had better things to do," she said once we were alone.

"That was the sarcasm talking."

"What do you want, Liv?"

"I want to take you two for ice cream."

"I don't want ice cream," she said and folded her arms across her chest.

"Too bad," I said. "I think you need to talk about whatever happened today."

"And you're volunteering to listen?"

"Do you really want to talk to Cassie about what's got you so upset?" She looked to the ceiling but said nothing. "I didn't think so. I suppose you could turn to your mother. There's a chance that she has the capacity for compassion, but honestly, I think you're stuck with me." She glared at me again, and I offered what I hoped was an apologetic and sympathetic smile. "Listen, there's an ice cream shop a couple blocks away. It's always busy, and they have a ton of games to distract Cassie so we can talk."

"I appreciate the offer, Liv, but I'm fine. Really."

"No offense, but I don't believe you, and I'd feel better knowing that Cassie isn't about to get in a car with someone on the verge of an emotional breakdown. I'm not taking no for an answer," I told her, remembering her efforts to get me to come to dinner at her house. "You might as well cave now."

"Fine. Let's go," she said, sounding about as happy as I'd been to submit to her stubbornness all those weeks ago.

I hoped I wasn't going to regret this.

CHAPTER NINE

Cassie divided her attention between her brand new blue-spotted stingray plush toy, the dregs of her banana split and the flashing screen of the tabletop Ms. Pac-Man she fed endless quarters into. This outing was costing me a fortune, and it wasn't even going to net me a goodnight kiss. But as promised, Cassie was properly distracted. If she remembered that her mother and I existed, she showed no signs.

I wished I could've joined Cassie. I would have rather mindlessly devoured dots and power pellets and evaded Inky, Pinky, Blinky and Clyde than sit across a sticky table from Mira, watching her hot fudge sundae melt to a soupy mess and feeling progressively worse about my earlier behavior.

"Are you sure you want to hear this?" she asked before looking around the tiny, crowded shop for Cassie. Assured that her daughter, engrossed in the finest entertainment the eighties had to offer, had no interest in what the adults were discussing, she turned back to me and just stared, not at me exactly but in my general direction.

Maybe she was second-guessing her decision to confide in me, or maybe she needed a minute to find the right words. Maybe something else prevented speech in that moment. I had no way of knowing, but I offered small encouragement anyway. "It's okay, Mira," I said, resisting the urge to lay a reassuring hand on hers.

"Have you ever heard gunshots?" she asked.

Speechless, dreading what she was about to reveal, I shook my head no. Mira, still gazing vacantly at something over my left shoulder, couldn't have seen it, but that didn't seem to matter much. She continued almost as if she was speaking to herself.

"I hadn't before today. They don't sound the way you think they will, but—it's the strangest thing—I still knew exactly what the sound was when I heard it."

"What happened today? Did someone get shot in your store?"

"In my department," she answered.

"Oh, god," I said.

"One of my employees. I saw her fall. Her body just crumpled, and then the guy who shot her turned the gun on himself and…I didn't see. Someone pushed me down, and there was another shot, and then everything was so still and quiet for…I don't know how long. It seemed like forever before the screaming started. And the sirens and…" Her voice trailed off.

"Oh, god," I said again. This time I did put my hand on hers. I'm not sure she noticed.

"She was only twenty," she said, focusing on me now. Tears ran down her cheeks, and I couldn't imagine how she hadn't fallen completely apart.

"Do you know…why?" I had no idea what I should be saying or doing. Really, what was the proper protocol for helping a possibly former enemy move past witnessing a murder-suicide? I didn't know, but I hoped talking about it would be helpful in some way. At the moment it was all I had to offer.

"Tina told me her boyfriend was the jealous type, but…" She shook her head, unable to complete her statement.

"Did you know her well?" I asked, hopeful that talking about Tina would be more beneficial than reexamining the day's tragic events.

"Not really." She swallowed hard and blew her nose in a paper napkin. "She'd only worked for me for a couple of months." Her expression brightened momentarily before clouding over again. "She was going to start volunteering with me. She said she was looking forward to it, but now…" She again drifted into stark silence.

"Volunteering?" Here we go, I thought, a topic that would move us further away from the horror and sadness she'd lived through and most likely kept reliving. And it would be a safe subject should Cassie decide to abandon her video game and join us, though a quick glance in her direction confirmed that wasn't an issue I needed to worry about any time soon.

"I work with an organization that helps cancer patients deal with some of the side effects of treatment, the non-medical ones, of course."

"Such as?" I asked. Though my earlier remorse reasserted itself and a healthy dose of shame crept in at the mention of cancer, I wanted to know more about the philanthropic side of Mira Butler. My self-flagellating curiosity aside, it also seemed to help keep her mind off uglier topics.

"The cosmetic side of cancer," she offered and further explained. "I do makeovers and teach women—and some men— how to use makeup to help them look more…like themselves." She hesitated as she spoke, as if waiting for me to judge her. I'd given her every reason to expect me to jump on her for thinking something as superficial as cosmetics could have any meaningful impact on the life of a cancer patient. But I just listened, nodded and felt increasingly worse about myself as she enlightened me.

"I know it sounds frivolous. Someone fighting cancer has bigger things to worry about than her appearance, but appearance impacts overall well-being. A lot of patients don't like going out in public. They don't want people to see them—"

"Probably because so many people see them as sick." I remembered how my mother became more and more reclusive during her ultimately pointless chemo. She blamed exhaustion, and undoubtedly the treatment wiped her out, but her hermit tendencies had never surfaced before friends and neighbors started looking at her with pity.

"Exactly," Mira said, and the ghost of a smile touched her face. "So I work with a whole team to help patients regain some confidence. I know that it doesn't really change anything. No one has ever beaten cancer thanks to a great makeover. But the people I work with seem to appreciate what we do. It's silly," she offered apologetically, "but it's something."

I couldn't believe how self-effacing Mira was being about this, like she'd done nothing more than hold the door open for a stranger. It was so much bigger than she was claiming. I couldn't say for sure, but I felt pretty confident that my mom would have jumped at the chance to be fussed over in Mira's "frivolous" way. She certainly hadn't received it from me. My focus (well-intentioned and misguidedly hopeful as it was) had been on making Mom better. Later, when the futility of that effort became clear, I tried whatever I could to make dying easier for her. I never really considered how her appearance might factor into her wellness. Even if I had, I'm not sure a makeover from her cosmetics-averse lesbian daughter would have done the trick. I felt like such an idiot.

"I owe you an apology," I blurted, surprising both of us. I hadn't even realized I was going to speak, but my lack of forethought meant I couldn't talk myself out of saying something that needed to be said.

"For earlier?" she asked, obviously not sure where I was going with this.

"No," I said then reconsidered. "Well, yes, that too, actually. I shouldn't have been so mean. But also for judging you. When you told me what you do for a living, I decided that you were the same superficial princess I'd hated in college. A cosmetics manager couldn't possibly be a person of substance, could she? I learned one thing about you and let that determine what I thought about you. Kind of ironic, wouldn't you say?"

As I spoke I had fixated on a stain on the tabletop. Cowardly though it was, I couldn't bring myself to look her in the eye while I confessed to being an ass. More than just apologizing, I was relinquishing my eighteen-year hold on righteous indignation—no easy task. But when I finished speaking and risked a glance at Mira, I felt some relief. Her expression, which fell somewhere between bemused and gratified, held no anger.

"You know, Liv," she spoke in a conspiratorial whisper, "you didn't hide your opinion very well, so this doesn't really come as a big surprise."

"To you maybe, but I was sure I was one of those nonjudgmental, open-minded liberal types. Unlike *some* people," I added, hoping we had reached the joking place.

She smiled, granting me further relief, then focused on pushing her ice cream soup around with her spoon. She hadn't even tasted her sundae, which was a confectionary sin in my opinion. The homemade ice cream here was about as close to home cooking as I ever got, and I hated to see it go to waste. She seemed to be in better spirits though, so maybe it had done its job just by being in the proximity of her sadness.

I wasn't sure what to say or do next, and I guessed she didn't know either. It felt strange sitting silently across from her, neither of us looking at the other one. She focused on the mess in her bowl while I took in the sights of the busy shop: the stark white walls with posters of various ice cream concoctions, the hordes of adults with their sticky children and the well-used video games. Cassie was still enthralled by Ms. Pac-Man, her original stack of quarters rapidly dwindling, signaling her imminent return to our table and the end of our private conversation.

We would be parting ways soon. They would go home, deal with the day's tragic events and then move on. I would go back to my fishes and Patsy and weekends with women like Tara. I might never see them again, and I felt something close to regret. I realized then that I no longer hated Mira. Stranger yet, I actually respected her. I might even like her.

"What are you going to tell Cassie?" I asked, breaking the silence and startling Mira, who looked a little confused. "About today," I explained. "She knows you're upset about something."

"I'll tell her that a friend at work died suddenly. Not a lie but not so much truth she'll worry every time I head to work."

I was struck again by what a good mom she was, and I almost told her as much, but my thoughts turned in a different direction before the compliment made its way to my lips. "What does Cassie do when you work?"

"Good question," she said. "My neighbors used to watch her for me. They have a daughter about her age. It was perfect."

"Was?"

"They moved in May, so Cassie's been spending a lot of time with her grandmother this summer." The thought of Cassie being regularly exposed to that much evil terrified me, but miraculously I kept my mouth shut. "But Mother has informed me that once school starts again she won't be available as often. Apparently she's been ignoring her responsibilities and plans to put an end to that soon. For a woman with no obligations outside of entertaining her rich friends, she's surprisingly busy."

"Does Cassie really need a babysitter?" I asked, congratulating myself on ignoring a chance to insult Mrs. Butler. "I would think she's old enough to take care of herself."

Mira frowned. "She's definitely mature enough to be left alone. It's not like she needs someone to tend to her needs when I'm not around. She actually does very well taking care of herself, and lord knows my mother is clueless when it comes to caring for other people." She frowned again. "I guess I'm more concerned about her having companionship, especially on nights when I work late."

I doubted Lady Stalin had the first clue about that either but bit my tongue. I was pretty sure Mira already knew about her mother's lack of warmth.

"I'll figure something out," she said and waved her hand in the air dismissively. "I have a whole week."

Just then the subject of our discussion sidled up to the table hugging her new toy and smiling. "No more quarters," she informed us, and though I would have happily provided her with another ten rolls just to keep that smile on her face, Mira and I had been talking for close to an hour. It was time to leave.

I walked them to their car, not because I thought they needed my protection. We were in a safe part of the city, and I was hardly a badass when it came to security. I just didn't know how to say goodbye, and I wasn't sure I was ready to head back to my empty apartment.

"Do you need a ride anywhere?" Mira asked as she fished in her purse for her keys.

"No, thanks. I've got my bike."

"I guess this is goodbye then," she said and jingled her keys. She seemed almost as reluctant to leave as I was.

The mounting awkwardness of the moment broke when Cassie threw her arms around me in thanks. I hugged her as long as I could, hating that this could be the last time I would see her.

Later that night, I sat in my living room drinking a beer and reading. At least that was the plan, but my restlessness meant that none of the words on the page made any sense to me. Every five minutes or so, I got up to stretch my legs. After half an hour of periodically pacing my apartment and rereading the same page and getting nowhere, I set my book aside and gave my full attention to the thoughts that had plagued me since Cassie and Mira had driven away.

I knew two things for sure: I liked Cassie too much to let her disappear from my life, and Mira was desperate for someone to look after her. And since I had the unexpected benefit of working from six-thirty until three, my work schedule meant I was available as soon as the school day ended. Under normal circumstances, I would flee the scene of any sort of childcare. I barely managed to take care of myself, and outside of the aquarium classroom, kids and I were immiscible. But for whatever reason, I got along with Cassie better than I did most adults, and according to Mira, she handled self-care better than I did. What did I have to lose?

Surprising myself for about the thousandth time that day, I called Mira and offered my Cassie-care services.

"What?" Her sharp response rang in my ear. I wondered if it was shock or disapproval I heard.

"I'm volunteering to stay with Cassie on the days you have to work late," I repeated. "I'd like to help you out." She was so quiet I wondered if she was still on the line. "Did I lose you?"

"Yeah, pretty much when you agreed to be our hero. Are you sure you want to do this?"

"You said she takes care of herself, so I wouldn't have to do anything. I'd just be keeping her company. I'm pretty good at that."

"I agree," she said. "Thank you. Again. For everything. You're single-handedly keeping my family from falling apart."

"You're welcome," I said, oddly delighted by her gratitude. I knew that, to Mira, this was an enormous favor from an unexpected source, but I really didn't have anything better to do most afternoons. Hanging out with Cassie would be more fun than sitting in my apartment alone. Really, she was doing me a favor.

"Hey," Mira intruded on my thoughts. "This might sound crazy, but do you think we could...maybe...be friends?"

"Mira, I think that's the least crazy thing I've heard all day."

CHAPTER TEN

Patsy took the news of my tentative friendship better than expected. Extremely loyal, fiercely protective and an excellent grudge holder, she didn't often dismiss her contempt for someone. She could sometimes be persuaded to offer second chances when the offending party proved him or herself worthy of reconsideration, but after that, nothing shifted her opinion. She adhered to a firm two strikes policy—neither patient nor forgiving enough for three strikes. Anyone who needed more chances than that to treat her well didn't deserve her time or energy. More than once I'd benefitted from her rigid refusal to forgive and forget, and usually I loved her for it.

In this instance, however, I wasn't sure where Mira stood on her register of offenses. Would she count Mira's less than satisfying apology as her second strike, or would it be considered a continuation of her first offense? I could see Patsy going either way, but no matter, the effort of convincing her to give Mira a second (or possibly an unprecedented third) chance seemed daunting but necessary. Not that I thought we'd all go out. She and Mira would probably never see each other. But my life would be hell if she thought I was being too forgiving or gullible.

However, when I told her about my arrangement with Mira, she actually seemed excited.

"You're getting a protégé!" She clapped delightedly at the idea.

"Excuse me?" My confusion sprang from numerous sources, and I hoped she would address each of them without endless prodding from me.

"Cassie," she explained with zero patience. "She's already caught the science bug. After a few weeks with you as her Nanny McPhee, it'll be a full-blown infection."

"That's so appealing. Thank you," I said. "Are you actually happy about this? You heard the part about being friends with Mira, right?"

"Yes, I did, and in spite of that, I think this might be good for you." I tried not to let my jaw drop. It wasn't a ringing endorsement, but we'd dodged the insult and berate portion of her feedback, so I considered the conversation a success. "It will get you out of the house for something other than work, women or trying to corrupt me," she added.

"You make me sound like a hermit."

"Not a hermit. Just predictable." She smiled sweetly. Then, apparently finished with my news, she moved on to telling me about her latest conquest—a twenty-three-year-old something or other in the Navy. She ignored my comment about her resorting to trolling the docks for a date but insisted on giving me more details about her encounter with her new boy toy than I even wanted about my own sex life. By the fourth time she referred to him as her seaman (with an accompanying wiggle of the eyebrows), I gave up all hope of having a mature discussion and said goodbye.

Perplexed but happy to face a judgment-free stint as Cassie's chaperone, I volunteered to start early. That way Mira's mother could return to her other obligations and quit giving Cassie insecurity boosts on such a regular basis. But Mira turned me down. Cassie and Satan Claus had planned a back-to-school shopping spree, an activity I had no hope of or interest in completing successfully.

So my inaugural shift didn't take place until halfway through Cassie's first week of school. We had fun, at least when she took breaks from her homework to tell me about school and her friends or to talk to me about fishes and the aquarium.

"Did you know that octopuses can learn mazes and solve puzzles?" she asked me.

"As a matter of fact, I did. Did you know they have three hearts?"

"And blue blood," she responded, reminding me that I'd have to work a little harder than normal to astound her with my knowledge.

At first I thought she was just testing me, trying to see if she could stump me. I've heard that teenagers can be smug and aggravating like that, but in her case, she genuinely liked learning and sharing information. This friendly quizzing soon developed into a regular form of communication for us, one that was beneficial for us both.

Even with the enjoyable distraction Cassie provided, it took me some time to stop feeling weird in Mira's house, even though Mira had done everything possible to ensure my comfort. In addition to providing detailed instructions for operating the TV, microwave, thermostat, fireplace and washer and dryer, she also offered snacks, drinks and several fish magazines (*Tropical Fish Hobbyist*, *Field and Stream* and a couple I had never heard of before) for my enjoyment. All in all, she'd set me up to have an easy time in her home with her daughter.

But the fact that I was making myself at home in Mira's house was bizarre to me. Aside from one slightly awkward phone call to discuss the specifics of our arrangement, we'd done nothing particularly friendly since our truce and friendship oath less than two weeks earlier. The only other time I'd been in her house had been a tense affair. Now, however, I was supposed to act like I belonged there and felt comfortable doing it. It wasn't easy.

Oddly enough it got a lot easier once Mira came home. She claimed it was an early night for her, though her arrival just before eight made me wonder if she knew what early meant. The door barely closed behind her before she asked if Cassie and I had eaten.

"If you count half a bag of pretzels and some chips eating, then yes, we've eaten."

She just stared at me. She didn't even need to say the words, "I don't" for me to know what she thought of my dining habits. Cassie shrugged when Mira looked to her for confirmation of our nutritionally empty meal.

"What about your homework? Did you manage to get that done?"

"Finished two hours ago," Cassie informed her.

Satisfied with her daughter's answer, she granted permission for TV, video games or whatever other amusement Cassie had in mind and then headed into the kitchen to rectify my dubious approach to dining. I took that as my cue to leave and started gathering my things, but Mira stopped me.

"Stay. I'll make you dinner."

"You don't have to." Things had been going more or less smoothly so far, and it seemed too soon to test the limits of our new friendship with a sit-down meal.

"Aren't you hungry?"

"Usually."

"Then let me feed you. It's the least I can do."

Mira, obviously better at this friendship business than I was, handed me a beer and launched into small talk as she gathered ingredients for whatever she planned to feed us. A flash of red caught my eye, but I paid little attention to her activities. Having already eaten at her house once, I figured anything she fixed would be a thousand times better than the nuked whatever that lurked in my freezer.

"How was work?" she asked as she moved about. She seemed unfazed, like it was a completely normal dinnertime activity for us to sit around her kitchen chatting while she prepared our meal.

"Great," I answered.

"And how was Cassie this afternoon?"

"Perfect."

"Did she give you any trouble?"

"Nope."

Her chopping slowed, and she was quiet for a moment, possibly trying to find a question that would elicit more than a one-word response from me. I didn't know if she was always this curious or if I'd caught her on an especially inquisitive day. Perhaps she was putting in extra effort to compensate for the rough start to our relationship, but I confess I didn't make it easy on her. It wasn't my intention to derail her efforts, at least not initially, but once I noticed how much my short, to the point answers exasperated her, I enjoyed infuriating her. It was fun watching her work so hard to wear me down, and I was also curious to test the limits of her patience.

"What about your childhood?" she asked.

"What about it? That's kind of a broad question." Of course my wordiest answer would be a non-answer.

"Where did you grow up?"

"The city."

"What neighborhood?"

"Uptown."

"Do you still live there?"

"No."

I smiled sweetly at her, and she sighed in frustration. Though she sounded impatient, I could tell she was enjoying the challenge of trying to crack me. The corner of her mouth quirked up in a half smile before she launched into the next barrage of questions—about my apartment, my hobbies, my parents, why I didn't drive, how long I'd known sign language, on and on. And each time she asked a question I challenged myself to answer in as few words as possible.

I finally relented when she asked what got me interested in marine biology—a subject I actually enjoyed discussing.

"*Jaws*," I told her. I could tell that she was close to popping a vein, so I elaborated before the aneurysm kicked in. "I watched it when I was a kid, maybe six or seven years old."

"Your mom let you watch *Jaws* when you were six?"

"No way. I was sleeping over at a friend's house, and we snuck into the front room and watched it after her parents were asleep. I was fascinated by the shark. I wanted to learn everything I could. After that, I was obsessed."

"Did your mom ever find out?"

"I told her." She stared at me again with that same I-can't-believe-what-I'm-hearing look she gave me earlier when she asked if Cassie and I had eaten. "I could never keep anything from her, especially when I was excited about something. So the next day when I said I wanted to be like Matt Hooper from *Jaws*, I pretty much ratted on myself."

"Was she mad?"

"I think she might have gotten angry if I would've reacted like a normal kid and just had nightmares instead of finding a career path. But she wasn't one of those moms who got mad all the time. She was pretty understanding about most things."

"What about—" She stopped herself as if reconsidering what she was about to ask.

"What about what?" I prompted when I realized she had stumbled upon a question she was actually a little uncomfortable asking.

"What about…being gay? Did you tell her that?"

"Almost as soon as I figured it out."

"How did she take it?"

"She asked if I was seeing anyone, told me she expected me to introduce her to any girl I dated, and then the following summer she took me to my first pride parade."

She looked stunned. "How old were you?"

"Fourteen." Her mouth fell open, but I had apparently rendered her speechless. I guessed she wanted to ask more, but being a bit bewildered by my unconventional relationship with my unconventional mother, she needed some help. "I thought I was in love with a girl in my biology class—Jillian. She was smart and pretty in a reserved, nerdy way, and she knew that girls could like each other as more than friends. I thought we had this amazing, magical bond, but after a few months, I realized the magic was all in figuring out that I was gay, that being gay was even a thing a person could be. She was an important part of that, obviously, but—"

"You weren't in love with her."

I shook my head.

"Have you ever been in love?" she asked.

"No," I answered honestly but incompletely. I'd never given myself the chance to fall in love. After Jillian, I was more fling-focused, and none of my romantic encounters could be considered a relationship.

"What about you?" Tired of talking about myself, I hoped to shift the topic to her.

"What about me? That's kind of a broad question, don't you think?"

"Touché," I said, trying to ignore her smirk. "I was asking if you've ever been in love, but that's a silly question. I guess Cassie's proof that you have."

I had been wondering about Cassie's dad for a while. In all the time I'd spent with her, in various locations and situations, I'd never met him, so I guessed he and Mira were no longer together. Still, I was curious.

"No, Cassie's proof that I had sex."

I was so taken aback by her frankness that I could only manage a feeble "Oh" before Cassie bounded in the room, wondering if dinner was ready yet. I wanted to ask more, but it didn't seem right to dissect her parents' relationship while she stood there. I let it go for the time being.

The food—some pasta thing with fresh tomatoes and basil—tasted better than anything I'd eaten in weeks, and even though Mira excused me from cleanup duty, I insisted on clearing the table and helping Cassie with the dishes while she checked her daughter's homework. It was cozy and homey, and aside from a handful of dinners with Patsy and her parents and siblings, the whole evening felt more like so-called normal family life than anything I'd ever experienced. I felt a twinge of sadness walking away from their house that night, and I was already looking forward to a repeat engagement the following week.

CHAPTER ELEVEN

In just a few weeks Mira, Cassie and I established a routine that benefited all of us. Two or three times a week, depending on Mira's schedule, I stayed with Cassie after school, helping her with homework as needed, which was less often than I distracted her from her studies with conversation and general nosiness about her life in and out of school.

One such distraction came at the end of September, about a month into my stint as the world's most superfluous, least qualified nanny. The aquarium, riding the wave of financial success from the contest to name Pup 824, decided to celebrate with the otter-adoring public by throwing an official otter naming party. For a small additional charge, visitors to the aquarium could attend the celebration and be among the first to learn the results of the election. The event was scheduled for the last Tuesday of the month from four to six. The team behind the campaign planned several activities—most of them educational—culminating in the unveiling of our otter's democratically selected moniker.

Cassie hugged me when I asked if she wanted to join me. I took that as a yes. Then, as it turned out, that Tuesday was one of Mira's early days. Since she was free, I invited her to come with us, and I spent the afternoon entertaining mother and daughter with otter-inspired, educational fun.

Cassie was disappointed that Cecil, the name she submitted, lost to Harry P. Otter, but all the other activities combined with a consolation treat from our favorite ice cream shop placated her. Her mother, however, was none too pleased with my signature spirit-lifting technique.

"Ice cream? Now she isn't going to be hungry for dinner." Mira glared at me after I filled Cassie in on my plan, and I tried not to squirm.

"But it's a special occasion," I pleaded. "And she seemed so sad about not winning." There was no turning back from my cool, fun babysitter faux pas, but I hoped Mira would see it as the well meaning mistake it was. I really hadn't meant any harm. I just had limited understanding of the rigors of parenting. From the look on her face, the outlook seemed bleak, and somehow I doubted the magical powers of ice cream would grant me instant forgiveness.

"Sorry," I added and offered the most sincerely apologetic expression I could muster.

"Next time, check with me first." Her expression softened into an almost smile, offering me some relief.

Happy to hear there would be a next time, I swore to obey her wishes. Mira smiled fully then and admitted she'd enjoyed the parts of the afternoon that didn't include me undermining her daughter's dietary needs. I'd enjoyed the day as well, especially since most of my visits bordered on the mundane. We'd become familiar and comfortable.

After that first afternoon when Mira discovered my knack for malnutrition, she always insisted on feeding us, whether by cooking when she got home or by preparing meals in advance of the nights when she worked late, sometimes past ten. On those occasions, I got to demonstrate my amazing microwaving skills for Cassie, and I ended up eating at least a couple of decent meals a week. The downside was that I started dreading meals at home, but I managed to score a couple of pity dinners with Patsy, who still supported the whole arrangement with Mira and Cassie.

On her late nights, Mira usually checked on her sleeping daughter before pouring herself a glass of wine and asking me about the day. Every time, conversation about the details of my mostly unnecessary role as Cassie's sitter slipped into other areas. That's how I learned that Mira's father had died near the end of her junior year of high school, leaving her with her increasingly harsh mother and without the refuge of her more fun and loving parent. In turn she learned I'd never even met my father. For all I knew (or cared) he could be dead too.

But we didn't always discuss such serious topics. We were far more likely to compare notes on movies, books and music that we loved. Though she had an inexplicable (and almost unforgivable) love of country music, we found more similarities than differences as we shared our favorites with one another. We'd get wrapped up either in defense of our preferences or in mutual appreciation of some beloved bit of entertainment, and before I knew it, I ended up lingering in her living room for a half an hour or longer. Once I realized how late it was, I always apologized for overstaying my welcome and made my way home, already looking forward to my next shift. But as the fall progressed, my departures came later and later, and I apologized less and less.

One night in November when Mira entered the living room after telling Cassie goodnight, she caught me admiring a black and white photograph on her wall, one of my favorite things in her house. The picture looked professional but not posed. A younger Cassie, maybe five or six years old I guessed, was curled up in a chair reading a book, her expression serious, her hair messy. It was natural and beautiful, capturing her intensity in a moment. It made me almost sad that I hadn't known her as a young child.

"That's my favorite picture of her." Mira startled me by speaking. She handed me a beer (a recent addition to our nighttime ritual) and returned her gaze to the framed picture on the wall. "Usually she shies away from the camera, but she was so focused that she didn't even know I was there."

"You took this?" I don't know why I was so surprised. Given the casual, candid quality of the photo, it seemed unlikely that it had been part of a session in a professional's studio. It was taken by someone who adored Cassie, and Mira was the most likely culprit.

She nodded. "I took all of these pictures."

I gave the photographs a second look and noticed that most of them, no matter the subject, had the same professional but unforced look as my favorite picture of Cassie. In almost all of them, Mira focused on people, and she had a talent for capturing them in genuine, vulnerable poses. She even managed to show her mother in a softer, almost pleasant light, an optical miracle if ever I'd seen one. There were a few scenic photos as well, but those too were more than postcard snapshots. She seemed to look beneath the surface of her subject matter, whether it was a person she loved or a place she considered intriguing or fascinating. Her photographs showed the depth I had only recently discovered in her, and I was curious to see more.

"Mira, these are beautiful. Why aren't you a famous photographer?"

"Thanks," she said. "But you have a higher opinion of my skills than most of the world."

I found it odd that others didn't appreciate her work at least as much as I did, but I had to believe her. I'd never heard her sounding so downhearted, and I didn't know what to say to her after that. Not only was I not in the habit of boosting people's self-esteem, but I also doubted she would believe any cheery comment I made in that moment. So I just stood there silently, drinking my beer and wondering what to do next. I guess Mira must have been equally tongue-tied because she did nothing to break the unusual but not uncomfortable silence between us. I was about to excuse myself when she finally spoke.

"What are your plans for Thanksgiving?" She looked at me expectantly, no trace of her earlier sadness present. She seemed excited about the upcoming holiday. I, on the other hand, hadn't done anything to celebrate Thanksgiving since my mom died. With zero culinary skills and no family to share the day with, to me it seemed like a pointless holiday. I usually worked late or went to a bar. Or both.

"I think I have a turkey pot pie in the freezer. It's probably still good."

"That's festive."

"I'll buy a can of cranberry sauce on my way home from work," I said to appease her.

"First, you have to work?"

"Fish don't care that it's Thanksgiving. They still need to eat."

"That makes sense. I hadn't considered that."

"Most people don't."

"Second, wouldn't you rather come here and enjoy a nice home-cooked meal with friends than go to your tiny, cramped apartment to eat a questionable frozen dinner by yourself?"

I wasn't sure how she had so effectively described my living conditions when she'd never set foot in my home, but setting aside her oddly prescient comment about the state of my apartment, she was right that, under most circumstances, I would choose anyone else's cooking over the processed delights in my kitchen. Still, I wasn't about to insert myself in her family's holiday. I didn't even feel comfortable doing that with Patsy's family, and they treated me like one of their own.

"I like my apartment," I offered lamely. She raised her eyebrow but said nothing, possibly because she was waiting for me to say something that wasn't beside the point. "I appreciate the offer, but—"

"But nothing. I hate the thought of you being alone on Thanksgiving. You should join us."

"I'm used to being alone on Thanksgiving. It's been that way almost twenty years," I said, trying to be polite about refusing her invitation.

"And I think that's long enough, don't you?" She just smiled at me. Something in her eyes told me she'd have a comeback for any rebuttal I tried to offer. But that didn't mean I had to give up so easily.

"Really, Mira, I'll be fine. You don't need to worry about me."

"Of course I do. Friends don't let friends eat alone on Thanksgiving."

Damn, she was stubborn. And I was running out of ammunition.

"I can't intrude on your family's dinner."

"You're not intruding. I want you to be there. After all these months, dinner without you will seem kind of empty. We like you too much to let you say no." She smiled at me, and I felt my reservations slipping away. "Liv, I'm not going to buy any of your excuses. So just accept it. You're coming to dinner." She folded her arms across her chest and hit me with a stern expression she'd most likely perfected in her role as a mom. No wonder Cassie was so well behaved.

"I don't want you to go to any trouble for me."

"What trouble? I'm already going to be cooking."

"Will your mother be there?"

"Yes, but most of her judgmental energies will be focused on me."

Certain I had lost this argument (and not at all happy about it), I sighed heavily. She just continued staring at me.

"You're sure it's no trouble?" I asked.

"None whatsoever." She smiled again. She must have realized she'd broken me.

"What time should I be here, and what can I bring?" I asked, shaking my head. I couldn't believe I was agreeing to this.

CHAPTER TWELVE

Though I initially regretted giving in so easily to Mira's pestering, my opinion changed as soon as I stepped into her house on Thanksgiving. The weather—cold, wet and miserable since morning—had cast a gloomy pall over the day, but she'd made her home a cozy haven. It smelled like what I imagined family holidays were supposed to smell like—turkey and baking bread and spices I had no hope of naming but couldn't wait to taste. And her dining room table was like something out of a magazine. Regular dinners with Mira and Cassie were casual affairs. We sat at the table, but on those occasions Mira never bothered with a tablecloth, napkins, candles or a centerpiece.

Mira (who apparently took Thanksgiving seriously) greeted me enthusiastically. For a moment it looked like she might hug me, but I deflected the likely embrace by holding up my offering of wine. She thanked me genuinely and then complimented my dressed-up-for-me jeans and turtleneck, an extremely casual contrast to what she wore: a snug, plum-colored dress with a hard to ignore neckline.

"Would you like more wine before dinner, Mother?" She poured Mrs. Butler a fresh glass and proffered the bottle I'd brought for her mother's perusal before handing me my usual drink.

"I suppose this will have to do. It's the best one can expect from a beer drinker," Gail said, not to me but to the thirty-dollar bottle of chenin blanc in her well-manicured hand. I'd spent an eternity at the specialty wine store a few blocks from the aquarium, pestering the owner with silly questions in my attempt to pick out (and justify the expense of) my contribution to our meal. It was nice to see my efforts met with such a gracious response.

Of course the archfiend was right, but the way she said it without acknowledging me or the trouble and expense I'd gone to for something I wouldn't even enjoy, set my teeth on edge. It didn't help that immediately after slighting the single most expensive beverage I'd ever purchased, she swept her eyes over my clothing, frowned, turned her designer-clad back on me and left the room—full glass of my inferior wine offering in hand. I swore I could hear the cries of orphans and the oppressed in the delicate shushing of her skirt as she passed from the room.

Normally I didn't care what people thought of how I dressed, but I had wasted forty-five minutes staring at my denim and T-shirt heavy wardrobe, trying to piece together an outfit that wouldn't incur her scorn. Why, I didn't know. She already hated me over something I couldn't change, so there was no reason to expect her to refrain from judging me for things I could control. I was as annoyed with myself for making any effort to impress her as I was irritated with the princess of darkness for the ugliness I should have expected all along.

"Can I do anything?" I turned to Mira, hopeful that I could hide in the kitchen with her.

She refused my offer to help (probably a wise choice) and sent me to the living room to reacquaint myself with the never charming Gail Butler before dinner. I tried not to interpret that as punishment for my earlier refusal to hug Mira. Thankfully Cassie had also been banished to the living room, and when she saw me, she clamped me in an excited bear hug (inducing a spastic twitching in her grandmother) before asking me if I knew that seahorses can see in two directions at the same time and then dragging me away to look at the DNA model she was building for extra credit.

The mostly convivial mood faded quickly once we gathered around the table. We hadn't even put our napkins in our laps before Gail said, "Mira, I could have provided the linens if I had known yours were so…rustic."

She scowled at the apparently inferior tablecloth and napkins. They seemed fancier than the paper towels I was accustomed to at home, but somehow I doubted the Mussolini of domestic propriety would appreciate that observation. She was too busy sneering at Mira's place settings anyway. "Is this Corelle?" she asked with a shudder.

"More wine, Mother?" Mira topped off her mother's glass. She'd sidestepped Gail's judgment with more civility than I could have mustered. Then again, she'd probably had years of agonizing practice. I realized that celebrating anything with Gail Butler could drive Santa Claus to punch an elf. Her insufferable condescension amped up almost immediately, but as Mira predicted, she bore the brunt of her mother's displeasure, at least initially.

Cassie praised the meal almost immediately, and I chimed in as soon as I swallowed my first bite.

"Oh my god, Mira. This is delicious."

"There's no reason to blaspheme," Gail snapped. She didn't bother to sign for Cassie's benefit. "The turkey is a little dry. You should have called the caterers I recommended." She pushed her plate of mostly untouched food away and reached for her wine.

Mira's face fell, but she said nothing. At first I thought she was holding her tongue out of undue respect for her mother, but when she uttered a barely audible "Of course, Mother," I felt sick. I hated to see her bullied by such a vile woman, even if it was her mother.

"Maybe you just need a more refined palate, Gail." I thought my comment might upset her highness. The woman obviously prided herself on what she considered good taste, and I hoped to rattle her just enough to alter the course of her invective.

She glared at me—the first eye contact she'd made all day—and I smiled sweetly in response. She couldn't possibly despise me more, and unlike Mira, I had no reason to try to get along with her. Why not give Mira a break and maybe have a little fun in the process?

"More wine? If there's any left, that is." I upended the bottle, spilling the last few drops into Gail's glass with a flourish. "You seem to have overcome your initial reservations about this wine." I winked at Mira and saw a glimmer of a smile.

The open hostility that flowed from Gail after that seemed disproportionate to my actions, but it didn't surprise me. I gathered she wasn't accustomed to being challenged, certainly not by a *laborer*, as she insisted on calling me. It was, no doubt, intended as an insult, but since I'm not offended by hard work, I welcomed her criticism with a smile. And while neither of us resorted to yelling or overt arguing, the adults all understood that the table had become a battleground. It wasn't pleasant, but as I'd hoped, I had effectively ended her attack on her daughter's self-worth.

After dinner, I found Mira standing in front of the sink, watching it fill. I wasn't sure how well she'd taken my antics with her mother, who sat in the living room sipping coffee and finding fault with everything in her vicinity. The smile Mira initially favored me with had gradually been replaced by a horrified expression as she silently watched her beautiful holiday meal turn into a contentious battle of wills. I hadn't meant to upset her—quite the opposite. I'd felt oddly protective of her and had come swiftly and stupidly to her defense. Now, confronted with her shell-shocked appearance, I felt a little guilty.

"Let me do the dishes," I said, bumping her out of the way and grabbing a soapy plate.

"Don't be ridiculous, Liv. You're our guest, and you worked all day."

"You cooked all day, which, if you ask me, is way harder than my job. This afternoon, I just had to show up and eat. Please let me earn my keep somehow." I leaned in for a conspiratorial whisper. "Doing something that doesn't involve your mother."

She laughed, alleviating some of my worry. "Fine. You win. I'll go enjoy a glass of wine while you and Cassie clean up this mess. But if you need any help—"

"We won't," I cut her off and shoved her toward the front room where her mother was waiting. She probably wished she could stay with us, and for a few seconds I almost pitied her, but not enough to trade places. I'd rather wash every dish in the city of Chicago than attempt a civil conversation with her mother. At least I had a chance of succeeding at the first option.

Just as we finished our cleanup, Lady Lucifer returned to the kitchen to collect her granddaughter. At Gail's command, Cassie was going to spend the night with her in Satan's lair in anticipation of their Black Friday adventure day. I didn't envy Cassie that much alone time with her matriarchal overlord, but she seemed excited as she headed to the car that waited to take them back to Highland Park.

I intended to leave as well. I knew Mira had to be up early for her own, very different Black Friday experience, and I didn't want to overstay my welcome, assuming I hadn't already. But after seeing her mother and daughter out, she closed the door and fell back against it, blocking my exit. It seemed she wasn't sick of my company yet.

"So, would you say this was your best Thanksgiving ever?"

"It's easily in the top five," I said and followed her back into the living room, where most of our nighttime chats took place.

"Really?" she asked as she sank into her customary spot on the couch.

She had good reason to doubt me. Washing a thousand dishes immediately after an indigestion-causing mealtime tussle didn't exactly sound like a recipe for a good time, but I meant what I said.

"Really. Mom and I didn't do much for Thanksgiving since it was just the two of us. This was nice, at least the you and Cassie parts. What about you? How would you rate this Thanksgiving?"

"Completely draining but there were some highlights."

She gave me a look that I could only describe as amused disbelief, with a healthy dose of tension, but there didn't seem to be any anger in the mix. That was a relief. I didn't want to press my luck, though.

"You didn't have to do that, you know," she said quietly, and even though I had a good idea what she meant, I played dumb. I didn't really want either of us to relive The Great Thanksgiving Free-For-All.

"The dishes? It was no trouble at all."

"Not the dishes." She hit me with an incredulous look that I was starting to know a little too well. "Earlier, when you... Nobody stands up to Gail Butler."

"I didn't really stand up to her. I just refused to lie down for her."

"Maybe someday I'll give that a try."

"I recommend it but probably not at Thanksgiving dinner. Sorry about that."

"Don't apologize. If not you, it would have been something else. Welcome to family holidays."

"Were they better with Cassie's dad around?"

She let out a sharp, bitter laugh, and I couldn't help myself. Even though this was obviously a sore subject and she'd already had a rough day, I pressed for answers on the topic I'd wondered but had been afraid to ask about for months.

"Tell me about him."

She stiffened slightly at my request. "There's not a lot to tell."

"There must have been something that drew you to him."

"Of course there was. He was handsome and charming, prone to grand romantic gestures. He excelled at sweeping me off my feet. He did everything right."

"But he's not around anymore. So what happened?"

"He died. When Cassie was two."

Her answer was like a slap in the face. I hadn't even considered it a possibility. "I'm so sorry, Mira. I—"

"Don't be," she cut me off, her voice hard. "His death saved me from an ugly divorce. It was probably one of the best things that could have happened to Cassie and me."

"Ouch." Another response I hadn't anticipated.

"I know I sound cold, but Cole made it easy to hate him."

"I thought he did everything right."

"He did, until I got pregnant."

"He didn't want to be a father?"

"I think he liked the idea of it better than the reality. He slept around while I was pregnant, which was bad enough, but when we found out Cassie was deaf, he blamed me for her defect. His word, not mine." I actually hadn't needed that clarification. I knew what Mira thought of Cassie.

"And you didn't kill him?" I asked. I certainly understood how Mira could despise the father of her child.

"I think I was holding out hope that the perfect man I'd married would return, but he never did. He wouldn't even learn sign language. What kind of bastard doesn't even want a relationship with his child?"

"One more thing Cassie and I have in common."

"I'm so stupid, Liv. I shouldn't have said that."

"Don't worry about it. You're not wrong, and it seems like Cassie's better off without her dad around." I'd never considered my dad in a positive light before, but now I started to think that an absent father was a better option than the selfish prick Cassie had ended up with.

Mira reached over and squeezed my shoulder. "I think maybe you both are. I was about to ask for a divorce when he died."

"How?" I asked. I didn't know why it mattered, but I hoped Cole Morgan had met a violent end.

"Car accident," she said, to my immense satisfaction. "I'm pretty sure he was on his way home from his girlfriend's house, so I like to believe the crash was some sort of punishment. It's as close to revenge as I'll ever get."

"Does Cassie remember him?"

"Not really. I've told her about her father's admirable qualities, and she has a good relationship with her grandparents, who are wonderful. She's their only grandchild, and they dote on her. They make sure to spend at least one weekend a month with her."

"It's good that she has them," I said and looked into her dark eyes.

We'd shifted our positions during our conversation, and now we sat so close I could feel the warmth of her body. I didn't move back to my corner of the couch. For one thing I didn't want to draw attention to our nearness, but also, I didn't mind being that close to her and gazing in her eyes. The look she gave me was anything but a tolerant, "I'm trying not to be rude and kick you out" look. She seemed almost spellbound. And that unnerved me.

"I should go." I jumped off the couch. Very subtle.

"Okay." She seemed surprised but took my sudden escape in stride.

She handed me my coat and walked me to the door, but as I stepped onto her front porch, into the blessedly cool, crisp night air and almost to safety, she stopped me with a hand on my arm.

"Cassie's going to be with her grandparents on Saturday. They're having Thanksgiving part two."

I smiled but said nothing to Mira, who was too close again. I started to feel claustrophobic even though we were outside.

"It gets pretty lonely here without her." She bit her thumbnail and looked uncertain about whatever she wanted to say. She was obviously nervous, but I didn't know why. "So I was wondering, if you're not busy, maybe you'd like to do something."

"Just the two of us?" That was probably the wrong thing to say, but I was surprised. Our entire relationship was built around Cassie, and I hadn't expected that to change any time soon.

"It doesn't have to be. You could invite Patsy if you wanted." She looked disappointed, which was another surprise.

"I'm sure she already has plans, so that means I'm all yours on Saturday."

Before I could react, she hugged me, one of those soft, lingering embraces that I usually avoid, and whispered how much she was looking forward to Saturday.

"Did I just agree to a date with Mira Butler?" I wondered as I made my way home.

CHAPTER THIRTEEN

Every year on the day after Thanksgiving, Patsy and I met in a bar so she could ask about my lonely, empty day and gloat about her family's celebration, which somehow always managed to surpass the previous year's festivities. She'd tell me about the Thanksgiving care package her mother made for me (that somehow never made it to me), then encourage me to join her next year. I'd politely decline, and then we'd drink and call it a night once one or both of us found a date.

Only this time my more eventful than usual holiday made for an especially snarky Patsy. I had expected her feelings to be a little hurt by my dinner plans, and had the night not ended on such a confusing note, I probably would have glossed over the details when asked about my Thanksgiving. But, as usual, I needed her help figuring things out, and that required a full, upsetting disclosure.

"Let me see if I understand this." She took a fortifying swallow of her cocktail before chastising me. "Instead of coming to *my* family's Thanksgiving dinner, which I've invited you to every year for the last fourteen years and which you've never attended, you accepted Mira's first-time invitation, got in a fight with her mother and somehow ended up agreeing to spend the day alone with your former enemy. You're not sure if it's a date, so you don't know what's in store or if you should try to back out of it, neither of which problem you'd be facing if you'd just come to dinner with my family as I suggested."

"That's about the gist of it."

"Just for that I'm eating your leftovers."

I nodded solemnly at her meaningless punishment and waited for her advice.

"Is there a reason you shouldn't go?"

"There are about a thousand reasons I shouldn't go, starting with, this is Mira Butler we're talking about."

I signaled the bartender to bring us another round. The drinks at Patsy's bar of choice were overpriced, but even if they'd charged twenty dollars a beer, it was a small price to pay for my latest therapy session with her.

"I thought you liked her now."

"As a friend. I don't *like her* like her," I protested too quickly.

"Please. If she looks anything like she did in college, then you've been wading through your own drool for months."

"Fine. She's gorgeous, even more so than fifteen years ago." If I was being honest with myself, even before Mira's eye-popping Thanksgiving dress, I hadn't been blind to her good looks, and though I tried hard not to notice, what little evidence I'd seen indicated she'd taken excellent care of her body. None of that mattered, though, since she was still a bona fide, card-carrying heterosexual. "But I haven't been drooling, and she's still Mira Butler."

"Meaning?"

"Meaning I couldn't do anything even if I wanted to. Which I don't," I added belatedly.

"Okay." She rolled her eyes and turned her attention back to her drink, apparently done with my drama.

"She told me I could invite you," I said to fill the silence.

"Kinky," she said and laughed. "But I'll let you be alone with your girlfriend."

"She is *not* my girlfriend."

"Yet." She laughed at me again. At least one of us found the situation amusing.

After my fruitless conversation with Patsy, I ignored the whole mess. As usual I didn't feel up to self-reflection or confronting my own problems, but my standard avoidance did little to curtail my nervousness. I had nothing to distract myself with, so my anxiety over my outing of an undetermined nature with Mira built steadily until our appointed rendezvous.

The following day as I trudged through downtown Chicago in the waning light of late afternoon, the cold air stung my face, and a tight knot of apprehension settled in my stomach. Mira asked me to meet her at Michigan and Randolph, a location that gave me little indication of her plans for the afternoon. I thought maybe there was a bar or restaurant where she wanted to spend too much money. Shopping also could have been a possibility, though I hoped she knew me well enough to understand how little I'd enjoy that. Had I known what she really had in mind, I would have taken a rain check until August.

"Ice skating? You expect me to go ice skating?" This was possibly the stupidest question to ask as we neared the skating ribbon in Maggie Daley Park.

"You don't like ice skating?" She sounded shocked, like I'd told her I hate kittens or chocolate.

"It's hard to say since I've never tried it, but I'm leaning toward no."

"Why?"

"For one thing, it's cold out here. I dressed for more of an indoor activity."

"Don't be such a baby. You'll warm up once you start moving."

It didn't pass my notice that, even as I protested her chosen activity, she steered me toward the field house, from which a steady stream of smiling, skate-clad winter revelers disgorged.

"Wouldn't you rather go shopping?"

"You want to go shopping?" Her disbelief was appreciable, even without the furrowed brow and wide-eyed stare.

"Or anything that won't end with me spectacularly humiliating myself."

"I'm sure you'll be fine," she said. Her dark eyes danced over me as she sized me up. "You look like a natural athlete."

My face grew hot, and I suddenly felt grateful for the icy wind—among other things, at least I could pretend that was the source of my red face.

"You're going to love it," she said and held the door open for me.

"Unless they make skates with training wheels, I sincerely doubt that," I countered as the crowd swept us through the door.

"Humor me for an hour, and if you aren't happy, I promise we can do something else, your choice."

"Forty-five minutes and you have a deal."

"Are you always this difficult?" she asked as we approached the young man working the skate rental counter.

"For you, I'm just a little extra difficult."

"It's appreciated," she said and paid the fee for the inevitable loss of my dignity on the ice.

The skating went better than I expected. Still, after shuffling along slower than a geriatric snail and falling twice, I gladly accepted her offer to hold my hand. I'm ashamed to admit that I held onto her longer than necessary. After our first painfully slow circuit of the crowded ribbon (during which time toddlers glided past us), I felt slightly more sure-footed, but I still clung to her. I convinced myself that clutching her hand allowed me more freedom to appreciate the scenery without focusing on my questionable balance. It was a flimsy excuse, but obviously I wasn't thinking clearly to begin with.

The other skaters laughed and smiled as they whizzed past us, unperturbed by the near-freezing temperatures and the likelihood of mountains of snow in our very near future. Equally jovial spectators roamed the path adjacent to the ice, some interacting with skaters and fellow onlookers, others in their own world. Not far from where we all gathered, cars sped down Lake Shore Drive, their lights an almost festive complement to the revelry of the Christmas season. At this point in the year, winter's offerings seemed more magical than depressing, and if not for the death trap footwear I stumbled around on, I would have been captivated.

"Are you ready to quit?" Mira asked as we neared our starting point, dropping my hand when we came to a stop.

"Has it been forty-five minutes already?" I swore we'd only gone around twice, and even as bad as I was, I didn't think I was that slow.

"No," she laughed. "But you look miserable."

"That's because this is next to impossible, but it's not complete torture," I conceded.

"From you that counts as high praise. Should we keep going?"

"I agreed to forty-five minutes," I said and pushed myself off the railing that had become my new best friend. She fell into place beside me and again offered her support, but I refused it. "No hand holding this time." I was determined to get through the rest of this day without making it any more date-like than I'd already allowed. She looked somewhat disappointed by my resolve, but it didn't last long. "Stay close, though, just in case."

She smiled, and we crept forward at our plodding pace. I doubted she was having much fun babysitting me, but she never complained. I guess my ice capades were more entertaining than I'd realized.

We made a few more trips around the ice, and not long before we quit, she slipped her arm through mine. I didn't know what motivated the move. I thought I'd shown marked improvement, and it was a clear violation of my earlier no hand holding proclamation (at least in spirit), but I didn't object. For those last few minutes, while I had an easy excuse to do so, I let myself enjoy the nearness of her, her warmth and surprising strength.

"Is this something you and Cassie do often?" I asked as we moved toward the exit. It felt good to have Cassie there with us, even just as a topic of conversation. It was familiar ground, unlike everything else about the day so far.

"She indulges her mother every once in a while, but she's about as big a fan of skating as you are."

"Smart girl. Does she ever ask to go for a drink afterward to celebrate not dying?"

"We usually follow up with a hot cocoa."

"I'm going to need something stronger than cocoa."

We stopped at a bar near Mira's house. Only slightly better than a dive, the place was starting to get crowded when we arrived. If we wanted to sit, we had to take a booth in the back. Considering what I'd already put my feet through, I opted for the booth, though the private, dimly-lit space was probably not the best setting for keeping thoughts of romance at bay.

Neither of us spoke much at first. We just sipped our drinks and watched the other bar patrons. All the nerves I'd felt earlier rushed back and subdued the functioning portion of my brain. It would have been easy to let alcohol loosen my tongue, but I made myself nurse my drink. I'd already embarrassed myself enough for one day. I didn't need to compound my earlier humiliation with drunken idiocy.

Mira, however, felt no such restraint. Her sipping rapidly turned into gulping, and before I finished half of my first beer, our waitress appeared with Mira's second martini. She'd already removed her coat when we sat down, and by the time her fourth drink arrived, she shrugged out of her sweater and unbuttoned the top three buttons on her blouse. I tried to ignore the spectacular view, but Mira, sliding closer in the booth and leaning against me, didn't make that easy. If I didn't know better, I'd think she was hitting on me. That was ridiculous, of course. Even though she'd made great progress since her narrow-minded college days, she was still straight, and there were at least twenty guys in the bar she could ensnare if she was looking for romance. There was no reason to think she'd look at me.

But then the conversation started.

"I'm so glad we're doing this."

"Getting drunk?" I asked and slid a bowl of peanuts toward her. They weren't much as a weapon against inebriation, but they were all I had.

"No, silly. Spending time together." She laid her hand on my arm.

"Right. Because we never do that."

"Not like this. This is different, don't you think?"

Her words started sliding together, and I had to agree that this was a new experience for us. However, sarcasm seemed to be lost on her at that point.

"Do you remember the night before graduation?" she asked. Even though I had a good idea of what she was talking about, I pretended I didn't.

"Not really."

"Come on." She turned and leaned toward me, giving me an even clearer view of her assets. "You don't remember telling me you want more than just any woman?"

I remembered it perfectly. Patsy and I had made the brilliant plan of drinking in every bar in Charleston that we'd never drunk in before. There were a surprising number of them, considering the size of the town and Patsy's love of alcohol. In the third bar we wandered into—a noisy, neon-covered, pop music infused haven for sorority types that I wanted to leave as soon as we entered—we ran into Mira and her friends. It was the first time I'd seen her since returning to school after my disgrace, and I was fuming. Spurred on by Patsy and a generous dose of liquid courage, I approached a surprised Mira and told her what I wished I'd said two years before.

"You think I want you just because you meet my 'not having a penis' requirement, but it takes more than that, Mira. So much more. I need more than just a pair of X chromosomes to satisfy me. I want a woman who's intelligent, funny, passionate and kind. A woman who's generous and beautiful. Who wants me, who gets weak in the knees at the thought of me and looks at me with fire in her eyes because she can never get enough of me. And you could never offer that to anyone, Mira, so quit worrying because I will never want you."

I hadn't given her the chance to respond. I'd just walked away, satisfied and hoping that would be the last I'd see of Mira Butler.

"You don't remember telling me you could never want me?"

"Nope," I lied again.

Either she didn't believe me, or she didn't care that I forgot. She slid her hand up my arm, and she was so close to me that we were breathing the same alcohol-infused air.

"What are you doing?"

"What do you think I'm doing?"

She moved to kiss me, but I dodged her. No way was I going to let her do this. It had taken so long to get to the place of liking her rather than hating her. If she kissed me and regretted it or, worse, blamed me somehow for seducing her, I wouldn't have it in me to find my way back to liking her again. I'd have to walk away. And I didn't want to walk away. I loved Cassie too much, and I was growing much more fond of Mira than I'd ever thought possible.

She grabbed my shirt in her fist, pulling me back toward her, and though I struggled to keep my distance, she overpowered me. Before I could escape again, her lips were on mine.

At first I just passively sat there while an alarming warmth spread from the center of my chest outward. But it didn't take long for my body to catch up with the part of my brain that was screaming at me to take advantage of the fact that a beautiful woman was kissing me. My hands moved to her hair, and I pulled her closer still, our lips parting as the kiss deepened. One of us moaned, and she shifted. I think if the table hadn't blocked her movement she would have ended up in my lap. Just the thought of her straddling me sent a shock through my entire system, and I growled in frustration. I pushed back, pinning her against the padded back of her seat as the kiss broke. I was about to move in for more when Mira, wide-eyed and flushed, slapped her hands over her mouth and ran to the bathroom.

"Well, that's a first," I muttered and went to check on my violently ill date.

CHAPTER FOURTEEN

Mira was a surprisingly manageable drunk. Embarrassed but not combative, she apologized repeatedly for her condition, but she never complained or made excuses. And at no point in the bar, on our lengthy journey home or even in the relative haven of her own bathroom did she appeal to a higher power to end her agony. She just accepted that being turned inside out was an unfortunate consequence of a martini-based diet.

When it seemed safe to leave the bathroom, she quietly thanked me for helping her and let me tuck her into bed. After the kiss she planted on me earlier, that wasn't how I envisioned ending up in Mira's bedroom, but I found myself more worried about her current ailment than upset about the disappointing turn the evening had taken. And though I hated to leave her alone, she hadn't asked me to stay, and that choice wasn't mine to make.

My situation didn't improve much the following day. I didn't sleep long or well thanks to my unrelenting thoughts of Mira. Given the condition she was in when it happened, I wasn't sure if she'd remember kissing me, but it wasn't something I'd soon forget. And not only because of the unfortunate conclusion. Kissing her had been exquisite, and though I couldn't say that her amorous assault had been inspired by anything other than four martinis in rapid succession, I hoped she'd feel inclined to try sober kissing in the very near future.

When I wasn't wondering what the hell happened at the bar and how to orchestrate a repeat performance (preferably without the vomiting), I worried about her and wished she had someone with her. I knew how much better it felt to be coddled and cared for when I was sick, and even though her current condition was self-inflicted, that didn't mean she should have to suffer alone. I knew Cassie would be home later that day, but precocious as she was, I sincerely doubted she knew her way around hangover remedies.

I felt drained before I got out of bed, and for a few minutes I wished I could be the kind of person who easily called in to work. I wasn't sick, but maybe I could call in emotional. Not that it would help me to lie in bed dwelling on my concerns. At least at the aquarium I'd have enough to focus on that I would stop obsessing over Mira. That was the theory anyway.

As it turned out, my exhaustion interfered with my focus almost as much as a certain brunette, who, I hoped, was still sleeping it off. In the end, only one thing at work came close to competing with Mira for my attention—Roman's standard (if tardy) email giving his thanks for all of our hard work during the year.

Normally I wouldn't find his customary offering of gratitude so compelling, but after his litany of the aquarium's triumphs—increased memberships, attendance and donations, other impressive achievements that actually involved the animals—he concluded the message by announcing a new position at the aquarium. *Expansion of duties* would probably be a more accurate term since the new Educational Director would still perform most of her or his tasks as an aquarist in addition to everything the new position entailed. The amount of work expected of one person seemed endless, but I didn't care. As soon as I read the job description, I couldn't help but wonder if the position had been created with me in mind. I'd already done much of the job on a small, sporadic scale over the summer, and the feedback from Roman and the board had all been positive. I could think of two or three colleagues whose teaching experience equaled or in one case surpassed mine, but if I wasn't a shoo-in for the job, I was at least in the running. It was an exciting opportunity, and it kept my mind mostly off Mira and the confusion of the previous evening for the better part of the morning.

At lunch, however, my relative composure ended as unexpectedly as it began. As soon as I sat down with my lukewarm vending machine burrito and my sixth cup of tea that day, my cell phone rang. Of course it had to be the source of my protracted inner turmoil. For half a second I considered not answering—though I had a thousand questions, I wasn't sure I wanted answers to all of them. I'd learned long ago that never inquiring was a great way to avoid unwanted information, but my concern got the better of me.

"I wanted to thank you for your help last night. I'm not sure I said it before you left." She spoke softly. Still I could hear how raspy her voice was. She sounded worse than I expected, and I wondered how rough her night had been after I went home. Maybe I should have stayed with her.

"Forget it. We probably would've had a similar experience in college if you hadn't been so mean to me."

I meant that as a joke, something to alleviate any awkwardness she might be feeling because nothing lightens the mood like dredging up the ugliness of the past, but she couldn't see my smile, and she obviously missed my playful tone. She groaned and sighed at the same time.

"I feel awful."

"Rough morning?"

She groaned again, and I pitied her, not just for her hangover but also for her lack of hangover preparedness. One benefit of my diet never progressing beyond college fare was that my kitchen was typically well stocked with good morning after food. Mira, however, actually cared about what she ate, so I doubted she had anything on hand that would help her condition. I could bring her a greasy, salty remedy after work, but that was a long time to wait for relief. I was about to suggest she order something when she spoke again.

"I meant that I feel awful about last night. That wasn't me."

"I didn't think it was," I said. I tried to keep the disappointment out of my voice. It wasn't easy.

"I'm so glad you understand."

"Of course," I said, my voice tight.

"I need to drink a gallon of coffee and take all of the aspirin before Cassie gets home, so I should go. But I'll see you Wednesday. We both will."

"Can't wait," I said and resisted the urge to beat my head against the table.

I couldn't believe I'd been so stupid. I'd allowed myself to think of Mira and romance together. I'd hoped for another chance to kiss her. I'd envisioned myself in her bedroom under far more pleasurable circumstances than I'd experienced the night before. I let myself believe that any of what I'd considered was plausible. What did I think would happen? We would go on more ice skating dates and make out once Cassie was asleep? Mira had no interest in me. At best she'd been curious, and thanks to a quart of vodka, her curiosity had been satisfied. And now I had to go back to seeing her as nothing more than a friend. Worse, I had to pretend I'd never seen her any other way.

I had no time to recover from that blow because almost immediately Patsy, awake just in time to enjoy the last half of her Sunday, called.

"I'm dying to know what happened. Was it a date?"

"No. I misread everything."

"I can't say I'm surprised, but I am sorry you wasted a Saturday figuring it out."

"Not half as sorry as I am."

"Cheer up, Liv." Her voice was far too bright and jolly, probably to compensate for my melancholy. "We should go out tonight and get you a real date."

I suppose it was better that she misinterpreted my tone. I could move past the Mira episode faster if I didn't have to dissect it with Patsy, which is without a doubt what would happen if I went out with her that night.

"I think I'm just going to stay in tonight."

In truth the thought of prowling the bars in search of a Mira substitute seemed unappealing at best. I hoped taking time to myself might help me sort things out, but time did little to improve my mood. I probably should have followed Patsy's example and just looked elsewhere for amusement and rid myself of whatever it was that had me so worked up over Mira. Instead, I brooded in my apartment every night until I saw her again.

I felt nervous all day on Wednesday, and for the first time since I met her, Cassie made things worse instead of better. Typically, on my afternoons with her, we spent some time catching up, our conversations about school, her friends and the aquarium delaying the start of her homework by no more than fifteen or twenty minutes. I looked forward to those exchanges with her as much as my late night talks with her mother, but that day I wished she would just go read a book and leave me to fret alone.

"What happened between you and Mom?" she asked me before I even had my coat off.

"What do you mean?"

"She's been in a weird mood since I came home from Grandma and Grandpa's house."

That didn't sound good. Was Mira angry? Disgusted? Depressed? Confused? What constituted a "weird mood" to a thirteen year old?

"She sent me to my room when I asked about you on Sunday, and this morning she told me that she might have to find someone else to stay with me when she's at work. Don't you want to spend time with me anymore?"

Tears shone in Cassie's eyes, and my heart broke to know that, even for a second, Cassie doubted that I adored her. If Mira wanted to send me away, or if, as I feared would happen, she blamed me for the events of Saturday night and didn't want me around her or her kid anymore, there wasn't anything I could do about that. But I refused to let Cassie think it had anything to do with her.

"I always want to spend time with you. Always. I wish your mom needed me here every day. I can't really tell you what's going on with her, but I'm not going away, not if I can help it."

In the short time I'd known Cassie, I'd learned to expect frequent hugs, so I wasn't surprised when she threw her arms around me then. What caught me off guard was when she signed an unexpected but not unwelcomed *I love you* before grabbing her backpack and heading to her room to study.

The fleeting joy of that moment with Cassie made the next few hours all the more agonizing. I had been so wrapped up in worrying about Mira and how the kiss would affect our relationship that, after my initial concern, I'd neglected to stress over the effect on my relationship with Cassie. Now I was doubly terrified and feeling extra rotten for my previous thoughtlessness. And I couldn't make up my mind whether to be more angry with Mira for bringing all of this about or afraid of going back to my old life. Three months earlier it had seemed so satisfying to spend all of my free time either in a bar or in some stranger's bed, but somewhere along the way I'd lost interest in bar and bed hopping. If Cassie was right and Mira sent me away, I didn't think I could return to my former life, not happily anyway.

I wanted to bolt as soon as Mira came home. She couldn't crush me if she couldn't speak to me, but I forced myself to wait while she checked on her daughter. It would seem weird if I ran out the door without so much as a goodbye. Plus, it wasn't like she couldn't tell me over the phone not to come back. If it had to happen, I'd rather just get it over with. By the time she finally joined me in her living room, I'd convinced myself this would be the last time I stood in that room, the last time I would see her or Cassie, and the last time I would feel a part of this little family.

She looked tired, like she hadn't had an easier time than me since we saw each other last—for somewhat different reasons, I was sure. She'd probably been hunting day and night for someone to take my place. Even so, she was radiant. Her tousled hair and finely sculpted features showed a vulnerability I'd never noticed in her before, and the change from her work clothes to soft, worn jeans and a loose, long-sleeved cotton shirt heightened her casual beauty.

"I should go," I said before she had the chance to kick me out of her life. I couldn't look her in the eyes and maintain my composure, so I stared at her bare feet. She'd painted her toenails a dark red.

"I thought we could talk," she said and leaned against the door through which I had planned to make my exit.

"I already know what you're going to say."

"Do you?"

I nodded slowly, still unable to make eye contact. I felt a lump of sadness in my throat, and I really didn't want to cry in front of her.

"Then I guess I don't have to say it."

She put her hand on my chin and lifted my face to hers. She was maybe an inch from me when I realized what was happening.

"What are you doing?" I stopped her just as I had on Saturday. I was so confused.

"Are you going to ask that every time?"

"Apparently."

"For a seasoned lesbian, you're awfully naïve about things." I couldn't believe how calm she was, like it was completely normal for us to make out.

"For a seasoned heterosexual, you're awfully eager to kiss another woman," I countered. As much as I wanted this to happen, I needed answers first.

"It wouldn't be the first time." She moved in again, but I put my hand up to stop her.

"Yeah, and you liked it so much last time that you spent the next two hours vomiting. I'm not really looking forward to reliving that experience."

"Because I drank too much, not because I kissed you." She had that raised-eyebrow, thrust-out jaw look of irritation she so often had around me, but I was dead set on discussing this. I would not survive another day of uncertainty.

"Let me ask you this. Would you have kissed me on Saturday if you hadn't been drunk?"

"I'm not drunk now." She ran her hands up my arms and through my hair, and I cursed my involuntary shiver.

"That doesn't answer the question."

"No, I wouldn't have." She stepped away from me and folded her arms across her chest. I felt the distance between us viscerally.

"Then why now?"

"I tried to explain on Saturday. I guess I didn't do a great job. I've been thinking about what you said the night before graduation a lot lately. At the time, I was angry, of course, then hurt."

Twenty-three-year-old me would have been ecstatic to know that, but thirty-eight-year-old me? Not so much.

"But now that we've gotten to know each other better, I feel something else when I think about it, about what you said. So on Saturday, I didn't kiss you because I got drunk. I got drunk so I could kiss you."

"What?"

"I needed some courage to do what I've wanted to do for a long time now."

"How long?" I asked, as if that was the most important part of her revelation.

"I don't know exactly, but if I had to guess—"

"You do."

"The night you told me about *Jaws* and your first girlfriend."

"Oh." I couldn't help it. I gulped.

We had inched toward each other as we spoke. It was so gradual and unconscious that I didn't realize either of us had moved until she was in my arms. Her lips—full and soft and perfect—were on mine, and she whimpered before her strong hands on my back tightened our embrace. She seemed ready to devour me, and I yielded completely. I moaned as our kiss deepened. My hands trailed across her back, up her slender arms, into her hair and briefly over her chest before settling on her waist. Like a more gratifying version of pinching myself to see if I was dreaming, I needed to feel her everywhere.

"You are really, really good at that," I said when our kiss finally broke.

She bit her lip and offered a crooked smile. "Do you still want to leave?" Her hands travelled up my back, but she made no move to release me from her grasp.

"I never wanted to," I told her and momentarily lost the power of speech as she nuzzled my neck. It seemed likely that she would be the end of me. "But I think I should go now."

"Why?" She looked hurt and confused.

"Because if I don't stop now, I'm not sure I ever will."

"How is that a problem?" She made a move to resume her nuzzling, but I held her off.

"I can't believe this is actually coming out of my mouth, especially at this moment, but I think we need to take the time to do this right. That won't happen if I stay."

"I'm not saying I agree, but how much time do we need?"

"I don't know," I admitted. "Maybe we should discuss it over dinner this weekend. Maybe on Friday when Cassie is at her sleepover."

"Fine," she agreed. She walked me to the door, and just before I stepped out into the frigid night air, she leaned close and whispered, "I hope it doesn't take too long" before tracing my earlobe with her tongue.

And if not for the freezing temperatures, I would have spontaneously combusted on her porch.

CHAPTER FIFTEEN

I couldn't believe how nervous I felt in the days leading up to my date with Mira. Never before had I ever experienced even a little anxiety before a date. What was there to worry about? At best the night would end in bed with the promise of more sex in the very near future. At worst, I ate one less meal alone. If things with one woman didn't work out (as inevitably happened, usually within three dates), there would always be another one soon enough.

But this thing with Mira—whatever it was—was obviously different from the whole of my romantic history. If the pre-date jitters didn't offer enough of a clue, there was my unprecedented request not to rush into bed with her. Two days later I still wondered how I'd found the resolve to stop what she'd started, but I knew it was the right thing to do. She seemed like the kind of woman who was meant to be in a relationship, not a tryst. She deserved someone who could offer commitment and stability, neither of which had ever been present in any of my previous liaisons. And that was just one sign that we were cursed from the outset. What about her latent homophobia or our turbulent past? Why was I even pursuing this? No one would win when this thing ended, as it surely would. Then she would be out a babysitter, Cassie would be robbed of a friend, and I'd lose Cassie and the only adult other than Patsy who meant anything to me.

If I had any sense, I would back out before we went too far. But contrary to what I'd told Patsy, I did like Mira—I *liked* her liked her, so I couldn't back out. And because "like" wasn't necessarily the most accurate description of my feelings for her, I needed to do this right, which meant doing pretty much the opposite of what I'd always done with women in the past.

I met her at her house, a risky move considering our last encounter in her living room, but meeting at the restaurant seemed indicative of fleeting interest, like the casual fling behavior I was trying to move away from. One look at her increased my nervous excitement (and not just on an emotional level). Her dress was criminal—somehow revealing at the same time as it left enough to my imagination to make concentrating on anything else a real challenge. Her bare shoulders begged to be caressed, and her long, shapely legs led my eyes on a satisfying upward journey to her spectacular backside (which I was immensely grateful I was now allowed to admire). She was stunning. She would be in sweatpants and an old T-shirt, but the effort she'd put into dressing for a date with *me* made me think that, maybe, this was more than curiosity for her. Maybe she *liked* me liked me too.

"Are you trying to make this impossible for me?" I asked when my brain decided to work again.

"Whatever do you mean?" She sounded innocent, but I knew better.

"I mean that I'm not going to be able to keep my hands to myself as long as you're in that dress, and I think you know it."

She leaned close to me, placed one hand on my neck, the other on my shoulder and whispered, "Are you saying you want me out of this dress?"

"I think what I'm saying is you look beautiful," I told her as I gently stepped away from her. My newfound resolve would fade faster than expected if she continued to be such an unrepentant flirt. "And if we don't leave now we're never going to eat dinner."

She reluctantly agreed to go, but she didn't make things any easier for me. She brushed up against me on her way out the door, though we weren't lacking for space. And her behavior in the cab not only made the driver blush, but it also left me with lipstick on my face and neck and necessitated a cosmetic touch-up for her. By the time we were seated at our table, I was done for.

Don't ask me the name of the restaurant or anything I ordered there—I was too captivated by my companion to notice much else. I don't even remember eating, but it didn't matter. I could have dined on clumps of grass and been just as content.

I couldn't help staring at her and wondering how we had ended up there. It seemed impossible. In the past I'd denied myself the pleasure of admiring her, an easy enough feat when I hated her. Then all I could see was her ugly inside shining through. As we'd gotten to know each other better, I still didn't allow myself to look at her like I would a conquest. Friends don't ogle each other, especially friends with the unfortunate history Mira and I shared. But somehow we had ended up in the last place I ever would have expected, and there we sat, in a cozy, dimly lit restaurant, gazing at one another across the table in a decidedly not platonic way.

As usual, our conversation flowed effortlessly, and even in the face of my distracting dinner date, I kept my wits more or less about me, at least until the end of the meal. We talked about work, books, movies, current events, pretty much everything except for the reason we were sharing that delightful moment. I thought we'd get around to it eventually. Technically, it's what we had agreed to discuss at dinner, but even if that hadn't been the plan, it seemed odd that neither of us commented on the fact that I now sat across the table from a woman who I hated six months earlier. The way we had slipped from a tenuous friendship into the start of a romance was bizarre. It really ought to have been a bigger deal, but I wasn't going to be the one to bring it up.

Mira must have felt as reluctant to approach the issue as I did because during the first tiny lull in our conversation, she brought up Cassie, our standard comfortable topic. I heard all about Cassie's weekend plans—her best friend's sleepover that night, followed by time with Grandma Gail. Since Mira had to work all weekend, Cassie wouldn't be home until Sunday night. I wondered why Mira hadn't asked me to stay with Cassie, at least on Saturday, but maybe Krampus in couture had made special plans with her granddaughter. And then, on the heels of her story about Cassie, I disregarded all of my dating survival instincts.

"Cassie's such a great kid. Have you ever thought about having more children?" Now, I knew better than to talk about babies this early on. Those tiny romance killers meant commitment, and even though I had decided to try things differently with Mira, this was not the way to go about doing that.

"I would have loved to have another baby," she said, a small grin appearing as she spoke. "But the opportunity hasn't exactly presented itself. I'm not sure it's a possibility anymore." She shrugged, as if to suggest she wasn't secretly pining for more mini-Miras. "What about you? Did you ever want kids?"

"No. I'm not good with kids." I doubt I'd ever answered a question so quickly in my life.

"Right. That's why Cassie hates every minute she has to spend with you."

"Cassie is different. She's perfect and impossible not to love. Pick any other kid, and it's another story entirely."

"You mean like any of the kids you want to teach at the aquarium?"

"Teaching kids isn't the same as parenting them."

"Agreed, but I think a little girl could do worse than having you as a mother."

Maybe she was right (except of course where meals were concerned), but the idea of me as anyone's mother was far-fetched at best. Unless it spent a good portion of its life in water, I had no business tending to any living creature. Mira clearly disagreed, and the way she looked at me as she contemplated my theoretical parenting gave me an unmoored feeling—not terror exactly, but not tranquility either.

"Have you ever considered getting married again?" I asked and immediately wished I could call the words back. This was even worse than the baby talk. Had any woman asked me about marriage (whether on the first, second or fiftieth date), I would have excused myself and never returned. Of course she wasn't as commitment averse as I was, but I was pretty sure that it was at least fourteen years too soon to start talking about marriage.

Not surprisingly, she looked somewhat taken aback by my question (maybe we were more alike than I'd realized), but she didn't dodge it.

"I suppose it would be nice to experience what I thought I was getting with Mr. Wonderful, but there's no guarantee I wouldn't end up with another dud. So barring a blood oath that it would work out, I'd probably say no." Safe as her answer made me feel, it also filled me with sadness for her and a healthy dose of anger for the fool who had mistreated her so. Before I could think of a safer topic to switch to, a crooked smile appeared on her face, and she continued, "Unless it was someone… undeniable."

I swallowed hard. Though it seemed absurd to think so on this, our first date that both of us were aware of, I couldn't help wondering if she meant me. Even stranger, the room hadn't started spinning at any point during all this talk of marriage. The remote and ridiculous thought that Mira might consider me marriage material caused the temperature to rise about five hundred degrees, but I didn't feel the impulse to flee the scene. I just sat there resisting the urge to blot my damp forehead with my napkin and trying to find a harmless subject to bring up next.

"Don't forget to breathe, Liv."

"What?"

"You look like you're about to have a panic attack."

"I was just, uh—"

"Thinking I was going to send out save the date cards before the waiter brings the check?"

"I'm sorry," I said and laughed at myself. "This is completely new territory for me."

"Dating? I thought you'd—"

"Dating with a goal other than getting laid," I clarified, perhaps more bluntly than necessary.

"Oh," she said, the word stretching out to infinity. I suspected she was starting to comprehend my preternatural gift for shunning strings and attachments. "So, have you ever had a relationship?"

"I guess." Conscious of the impression I was about to make on her, I looked away from her and fidgeted with my silverware.

"How many would you say you've had?"

"Including my girlfriend when I was fourteen?" I asked, stalling. She nodded. "One."

"You haven't dated anyone since you were fourteen?"

"No, I've dated plenty. It's just that nothing has...stuck."

"Are you worried this won't stick?"

"Terrified," I admitted. I hadn't meant for all of this to come tumbling out over dessert, but it was better if she knew what she was in for. I hoped I wasn't scaring her off.

"And that's why we're going slow."

I nodded, relieved that she understood.

"But we will have sex eventually?" The look she gave me would have sent casual sex me scrambling to pay the bill and find someplace private.

"Sooner than you think if you keep looking at me that way."

Her smile, even more than the smoldering look she'd just hit me with, told me that my recently discovered willpower wasn't long for this world.

CHAPTER SIXTEEN

I spent the following day driving myself crazy by replaying my date with Mira, but what started off as a pleasant excursion into the recent past gradually turned into me second-guessing myself. For the first time in pretty much ever, I had removed sex from the dating equation, and I had enjoyed one of the best nights of my life. It seemed logical, of course, since I'd enjoyed so much of my time with her before we started making out that I wouldn't suddenly need to have sex with her to have a good time. Whether it was her or the time spent getting to know one another that improved the outcome of a sexless evening, I didn't know, but the fact that I'd spent more time reminiscing about one date with her than all of my previous encounters combined told me that something good was happening.

Mira, more understanding than I could have hoped, seemed to support my need to proceed cautiously. At her suggestion, we'd walked back to her house after dinner, though the night was chilly and she wore heels. The partial moon hanging in the cloudless sky softened the city around us, making the perfect romantic backdrop for our stroll. As we walked through the neighborhood streets, she held my hand but otherwise attempted none of her earlier seduction, and when she rested her head on my shoulder as we waited to cross a busy street, the sweetness of the moment affected me almost as powerfully as her super vixen antics before dinner. I couldn't believe how satisfying it was just to be with her, satisfying in ways I hadn't considered before.

We stood on her front porch for a charged minute before she hesitantly invited me in, as if she didn't want to unduly tempt me. How could she not know that just looking at her could send me over the edge? I was nowhere near ready for our time together to end, so temptation be damned, I followed her inside. I rubbed her poor, high heel-battered feet for a time before she found *White Christmas* on the classic movie channel. Then for the rest of the night, we half-watched old holiday movies and made out like teenagers in her darkened living room. And instead of me sneaking out after she fell asleep, we shared a lingering goodbye around two o'clock. I left then only because I didn't see any benefit to Cassie returning home from her sleepover to find her mother and me in a compromising position on her living room couch. It had been a sweet, exciting, practically perfect night, one I was uncharacteristically reluctant to end.

But now that I kept reliving it, I began to wonder if I was doing the right thing, if waiting for what we both seemed to want was really the best option for us. Certainly the tantalizing build-up to the bedroom was intoxicating, like foreplay for days, but it couldn't last indefinitely. Even if I waited a year to sleep with her (an eventuality that seemed as likely as a walrus climbing a tree), I would still doubt what was happening. I'd question the strength of our connection and her interest, and I'd worry she would destroy my life yet again. Soon the fond memories I turned over in my head started to include a healthy dose of torment and uncertainty. Somewhere in the middle of my five hundredth trip down Super-Hot Date Memory Lane, a text from Patsy interrupted my worry-infused thoughts.

Drinks tonight. Meet me at eight. She followed up with the address of a bar in Boystown.

I considered refusing. Though the likelihood of me having a worse time in a bar with Patsy than sitting at home torturing myself with doubt seemed minimal at best, I wasn't in a particularly social mood. But before I even had a chance to reply, she texted again. *You WILL be there.*

It was like she knew I was reluctant to go out, which was weird because as long as I'd known her, I had almost never declined one of her invitations. In the past, drinking with her had been like a second job for me, one that, admittedly, had been far from lucrative, so I knew that it would be more fun than fanning the flames of my paranoia and trying not to text Mira while she worked.

Still, I had reservations beyond my hope that Mira would leave work early and call me for another marathon make-out session. I wasn't ready to tell Patsy about Mira yet. For one thing she was bound to give me a hard time just for attempting to have a serious relationship, but add Mira to the absurdity of me and commitment sharing the same space, and it would be a bloodbath. Evasive maneuvers were my only hope, but I had no legitimate excuse to refuse Patsy's invitation. Even if I offered one, she'd wear me down eventually. It was easier to agree right away. So if I wanted to end the night with Patsy in the dark about my strange new romance, that meant my options were lying (which I stank at) or trying to avoid the topics of women, dating and sex (a near impossibility when I combined booze and time spent with Patsy). Certain she would kill me before the night ended, I agreed to meet her and hoped for a swift end to my misery.

The club she picked catered mostly to gay men, which I thought an odd choice for her. She wasn't typically one to satisfy herself with eye candy alone. I hoped it would work in my favor, though. With fewer one-night stand prospects for both of us, it would be easier to keep the conversation away from illicit liaisons without being obvious that that's what I was doing. Unfortunately, she thought the handful of women present were deserving of my affections, and almost from the moment we walked in the door, she started directing my attention to the female population of the bar.

"Look at her." She hitched her chin in the direction of a pretty enough blonde lingering near the bar, waiting for some willing fool to refresh her drink.

"Why is she so tan? It's December."

"You should ask her. Maybe she'll show you her tan lines."

"I'll pass," I said and made my way to the other end of the bar to get us drinks.

By the time I returned, she'd zeroed in on another prospect for me—an adorable youngster who had fully embraced the advice to dance like nobody was watching.

"Did she come here on a school bus?" I asked, vetoing bachelorette number two.

Undeterred, she pointed out two more women before I finished my first beer. I shot down both of her recommendations, and I could almost see her frustration as I pointed out each woman's negligible deficiencies. I'd never been this picky in the past, but in the past I hadn't been fixated on a gorgeous brunette currently stuck at work.

"How about that one?" She gestured at a woman laughing with a small group of lesbians in the corner. She had dark hair like Mira's but was shorter and hadn't been blessed with Mira's full lips. I couldn't help smiling at the image of Mira that this stranger had conjured in my mind, and Patsy, misinterpreting my grin, urged me on. "You should go for it."

"I'm not really interested."

"What could possibly be wrong with her? Are her teeth too straight? Is her hair not brown enough?"

"I'm not in the mood," I answered.

"So get in the mood! Are you seeing what I'm seeing? This is not an opportunity to pass up." She stared at me, understandably confused.

"If you like her so much, why don't you hit on her?"

"I can't."

"Why not? I thought this wasn't an opportunity to pass up."

"I'm seeing someone." She looked around the bar, avoiding eye contact.

"Like a therapist?" As soon as I said it, I realized my mistake.

She glowered at me. "I'm in a relationship. With Alex." She said it like it was the most natural thing in the world for her to be dating someone exclusively and like I should know who Alex was.

"So Alex is your…" I didn't know whether to say boyfriend or girlfriend. Either one was a possibility, though they both seemed unlikely. This was Patsy, the only person less inclined to commitment than me.

"*He* is my boyfriend."

"Since when?"

"Late September."

"You're not seeing anyone else?"

"Isn't that what having a boyfriend means?" She raised an eyebrow and glared at me.

"To most," I answered. I was dumbfounded. Of all the ways I thought this night would go, finding out that Patsy had been seeing the same person—singular—for more than two months was not one of them. How had we both stumbled into what, for us, passed for romantic stability at the same time?

"And you didn't tell me until now?" I was a little hurt, though I didn't have much right to be.

"I kept thinking I'd get bored and move on, but that hasn't happened."

"That makes sense." While I wasn't worried I'd get bored with Mira, the nagging doubt sounded all too familiar. Still, as long as this Alex character was a decent human being and made her happy, I hoped it worked out. "Congratulations."

"You're not going to say anything else?"

"When do I get to meet him?"

She slumped back in her chair, her relief evident. "You're really not going to make fun of me for this?"

"I wouldn't dream of it." Her raised eyebrow hit new heights, and I knew she knew I was hiding something.

"What now?" she said and immediately tensed, like she was bracing herself for whatever preposterous thing was about to fly out of my mouth.

"It's nothing, really. It's just that—" I swallowed hard, wondering if I was about to make a gargantuan mistake. "I'm dating Mira." I spoke the words in a rush, as if the speed of my confession would make it more palatable.

Even though her situation ought to make her more understanding, I still feared her reaction to my news. It wasn't every day her lady lothario best friend fessed up to having feelings for one woman, let alone the one woman she'd years earlier sworn to hate forever. But Patsy deserved the truth. Her mouth fell slightly open and she blinked at me for several minutes, but otherwise she took it fairly well.

"I thought you were wrong about that."

"I was wrong about being wrong," I said and told her everything, from Liv and Mira's Adventures on Ice all the way up to our date the previous night. Her stunned expression gradually receded as she listened to the details.

"Mazel tov," she said when I finished.

And that was it. We spent the next few hours sharing details of our respective romances, but neither of us ever came even remotely close to judging the other one. Her calm response surprised me, but I wasn't about to press her for a more thorough opinion of my relationship. I wondered if she would have been as receptive if not for her boyfriend, but again, I decided not to question it. Instead, I savored the relief I felt.

I had told my best friend my big secret, and she hadn't tried to stage an intervention. I had worried about telling her for nothing, and if I had been so wrong about her reaction, maybe I was wrong to worry about other things as well.

CHAPTER SEVENTEEN

Time dragged at work on Sunday, probably thanks to my exhaustion—an unnecessary reminder that I'd stayed out too late drinking with Patsy. I'd somehow escaped a hangover, but while we sat at the bar discussing the improbability of both of us settling down at the same time, I'd also missed a call from Mira. She wanted to let me know that she was home from work, and her voice slipping into a low, seductive register that tightened my stomach, she added that *Christmas in Connecticut* would be airing later that night.

I knew she'd never seen the Barbara Stanwyck classic, and I wanted to be there to introduce her to one of my favorite holiday films, though considering the way we watched movies together, she probably wouldn't see most of it. I doubted that would bother her any more than it would me, but Patsy would have been livid if I'd ditched her to go make out with Mira. It was better that I didn't know about the call until it was too late to do anything but text an apology to her and wish her a goodnight. Then I listened to her message again just to hear her voice.

Pathetic as I was, I replayed it a few more times the next morning before heading to the aquarium and on each of my breaks. After I clocked out, I was about to listen to the message one last time before deleting it when the object of my pining called. She probably knew I was elated to hear from her, just by my voice, which sounded mushy to my own ears. Thankfully no one else was around to witness me in my schmaltzy glory.

"I missed you last night," she said.

"Not even half as much as I missed you," I replied and wondered when emotionally detached me had been replaced by the sentimental fool now talking to her.

"Cassie wants to ask you something," she said after our sappy greeting. "In person. Tonight if possible."

"Are you using your daughter as an excuse to see me?"

"Are you suggesting I need to trick you into coming over?"

"We both know that's not true," I said. "What time does Cassie want me to be there?"

"She's thinking six."

"Tell her I'll see her then."

"She can't wait. Neither can I," she said, and feeling mushy again, I headed home for a much needed shower.

Cassie snagged me as soon as I arrived and enlisted my help in setting the table. As we passed through the kitchen, I waved hello to Mira, and admiring the fit of her jeans, I wished I could offer a more thorough greeting, but Cassie was on a mission and paused just long enough to grab plates and silverware. Then I got to work on the table while she filled me in on the reason I'd been summoned to her house.

"My school is having a career day in February," she told me. I suspected I knew what was coming next. "They did it last year, too, and it was awful, mostly men with boring jobs like banking."

"Definitely boring," I agreed.

"So I went to my principal and told him that this year he should include more women with cool jobs and that he should invite you to speak. Then career day would be fun, and the other girls at school would like science, too."

I hadn't exactly anticipated that. I thought she would ask me to be a part of career day, but I never would have expected to hear that she tried to strong-arm her principal into putting me on the guest list. I don't think I'd ever met a kid so unafraid of asserting herself. She amazed me, and if her principal contacted me, I would be at her school's career day, no matter what.

"What did your principal say?" I asked.

"He said he'd consider it. That's usually adult talk for no, but I'll to try to convince him anyway. That's why I wanted to know if I can give him your contact information, just to encourage him."

"Absolutely," I told her and hugged her before we headed back into the kitchen for the rest of our table-setting supplies. I congratulated myself for starting to get the hang of showing genuine affection.

Mira made the perfect cold weather Sunday night meal—melt in your mouth pot roast with potatoes and carrots. I even liked the asparagus, and not for the first time, I wished she could feed me every night. Over dinner Cassie told us about her weekend away from home. She shared the details of her sleepover, with its requisite gossip, bra freezing and discussion of cute boys, a new subject for Cassie, based on Mira's wide-eyed reaction. Cassie had also managed to have fun with her grandmother (a point as startling to me as the news of Cassie's boy craziness had been to Mira). She radiated joy as she told us of their trips to three different museums, including one of the last places I would expect Gail Butler to willingly appear—the inelegant, hands-on paean to the working class Museum of Science and Industry. And though I gave Cassie my mostly undivided attention, throughout her story, I stole glances at Mira. Every time our eyes met, my chest constricted, my vision blurred, and I wished Cassie were still with her grandmother so I could have my way with Mira. As it was, I doubted I could wait until Cassie went to bed to get my hands on her mother.

Something had shifted in me since I last saw Mira. Maybe because Patsy, who knew me better than anyone, hadn't immediately proposed an exorcism or called me delusional for even considering a relationship and had actually seemed to think commitment was possible for me, I felt more confident about my connection to Mira. And right then I was having trouble focusing on anything other than the inviting neckline of her soft gray sweater and all the ways my mouth could delight us both in just that patch of gloriously exposed skin, not to mention what my hands might do in the meantime. But it seemed wrong to ravage her while her daughter munched on carrots and told innocent stories of adolescent girls and an atypically kind grandmother. So instead I sat there wishing Cassie would wrap things up and go to bed, hating myself for the thought.

By the time she finally called it a night (an hour later than usual since she'd neglected much of her homework over the weekend), the air between Mira and me was charged. We'd been sitting on opposite ends of the couch, carefully keeping our hands to ourselves while we waited for Cassie to tell us goodnight, but while we'd refrained from physical contact, we'd scarcely looked away from one another. For over an hour, I'd taken in every inch of her, letting my imagination unravel the mystery that lay beneath her clothing and trying to decide where I wanted to kiss her first. Every option seemed perfect, and even after Cassie went upstairs to bed, I had yet to settle on the most exquisite route along Mira's body. When my glance returned to her face, I caught her staring at my mouth. I licked my lips and looked into her heavy-lidded eyes, certain her thoughts mirrored my own.

"You should probably check on your daughter," I said, my voice low.

"Why is that?" Her innocent tone, belied by the crooked half-smile that appeared on her face, didn't fool me. She knew exactly why. She wanted to hear me say it.

"Because," I moved toward her, "she really shouldn't see anything I'm about to do to you." I kissed her fiercely then, thrilling at her low moan when I caught her bottom lip between my teeth.

"You aren't still worried that it's too soon?" Concern partially shrouded the desire in her eyes.

"The only thing I'm worried about right now is not being able to restrain myself long enough to get upstairs." I kissed her again for emphasis and let my hand trail lightly up her arm to her throat and then downward, pausing briefly at her cleavage.

"Oh." Her breath hitched, and her lips parted. "All right then." She grabbed me by the hand. "Cassie's room is on the way to mine. You should follow me."

Anywhere, I thought. I didn't know how I managed to keep that to myself.

The light from the hall filtered through the half-open door to Cassie's room, just reaching her bed. She clutched her stuffed stingray, and her angelic face, so peaceful as she slumbered, gave me a moment's pause. As far as I knew, I'd never slept with anyone's mom before, certainly not while the kid slept two doors away.

"Is this all right?" I asked Mira as she smiled at her sleeping daughter.

For an answer she pulled me into her room and closed the door. She kissed me hard, picking up where we left off on the couch.

"It's been over three years since Cassie woke up in the middle of the night needing her mother. We should be alone for a while." She kissed me again, pressing herself against me.

"And are you sure you want this?" I thought I knew the answer, but I needed to be certain. "This will change everything."

"Maybe I need things to change," she said.

Her eyes flashed as she stared at me, her lips slightly parted and her breathing slow and heavy. My chest rose and fell with hers, and before I could fabricate another doubt or excuse, before I could talk myself out of what I wanted, I tightened my arms around her and kissed the hollows of her neck and collarbone. Her skin was so soft, and I felt the vibration of her satisfied "Mmm" against my tongue.

My hands moved under her sweater, raking across the smooth planes of her back before moving around to cup her breasts. Even through her bra I could feel her nipples respond, and it was my turn to groan as I pulled her sweater over her head and stepped back to admire her. She unfastened her bra, letting it fall to the floor moments before I went to my knees in front of her to kiss her flat stomach and caress her everywhere I could reach. Her bare breasts—so perfect in my hands—her hips and long, lean thighs, so strong and feminine. Nothing I had imagined came close to the beauty of the woman before me.

Overcome with desire, I opened her jeans and with a sudden ferocity, pulled them and her pink panties down. As she stepped out of the clothes at her feet, the scent of her arousal hit me. I swallowed hard and rose. With a surprising strength considering my weak and trembling legs, I carried her the short distance to the bed. She wrapped her bare legs around me and even through my shirt, I knew she was ready for me. Our mouths never parted, and once we fell upon the cool, soft sheets, my thigh between her legs, she rocked against me. My hands moved to her breasts, and a low moan escaped her when my mouth took over, teasing first one nipple and then the other with my teeth and tongue.

She'd gotten me out of my shirt somehow. She didn't get to my bra before I moved out of her reach on my slow descent of her torso. I kissed her abdomen and navel, down one heavenly thigh to her calf and then ran my tongue from the back of her other knee, up the inside of her thigh, finally settling between her legs. She opened herself and moaned again as I tasted her, gently at first, then with the full force of my yearning. For several exquisite minutes, I studied her, learning what she liked best by her movements, her breathing and her hands in my hair. Too soon, her hips rose from the bed as she gripped my hair, and her voice, husky and low, purred my name.

I should have been sated, but her tousled hair, her flushed skin and the erratic rise and fall of her chest reignited the desire within me. Not even close to satisfied, I moved back to her breasts, loving the contrast of soft flesh and firm nipple against my tongue. She writhed beneath me as I teased her and trailed my hand along her torso. Then her long "Ohhh" rang in my ears, and she wrapped her legs around me again as my fingers opened her and slipped inside. She met my slow, firm strokes with thrusts of her hips, holding off her orgasm as long as possible. But when I brought my other hand to her, gently stroking that one sensitive bundle of nerves, she shuddered beneath me. I felt her contractions gripping my fingers, and I almost lost control at the sound of her guttural moan.

"How?" she asked breathlessly a few minutes later. "How am I naked and spent, and you still have most of your clothes on?"

I smiled and kissed her, still wanting more. But she pushed me onto my back and straddled me. Before I knew it my bra had been discarded, and her hands were on my breasts with none of the hesitation I expected from her. She knew what she wanted and took it.

In short order, she flung my pants to the floor, my panties immediately following. Her hair fell around our faces as she leaned forward to kiss me and grind against me. That alone could have been my undoing, but then her mouth came to my nipple, and I whimpered. She kissed me again, her tongue plunging into my mouth. Then she was gone. The cold air touched my overheated skin, and I worried she'd panicked and changed her mind.

Then her breath and her tongue fluttered along my thighs, and her mouth was on me. I groaned and lost the power of speech as she grasped my hips, pulling me closer to her. She teased and lingered in all the right places, her focus and aptitude beyond admirable. Almost embarrassingly soon, I saw stars, and I cried out her name as my hips bucked, lifting both of us off the bed.

As she settled beside me, I kissed her with more affection than passion and wrapped my arms around her. Her hand moved lazily across my breast, and when she draped her leg across me, pressing herself against my hip, I felt how much she'd enjoyed what had just happened.

"Was that...okay? Did I do it right?" I couldn't believe she had to ask.

"You definitely didn't do it wrong. It was perfect," I said and kissed her forehead. "It's like you're a real lesbian now. What will your poor mother say?"

"Is that what I am?"

Despite the clear signals of her body language, I found her words troubling. I guess she wasn't exclusively gay, but she'd just engaged in pretty much the most lesbian activity possible (except maybe for playing softball), so what was she saying? I didn't want to push her, but I also wanted to know what we were doing. I *needed* to know. At the same time, I was terrified to hear her answer. If it was just sex she wanted, I could handle it. I'd had plenty of practice in the just sex department. Still, the thought of something so empty at this point seemed depressing.

"I guess bisexual would be the more accurate term, but do you really think someone like your mother would care about such distinctions?"

"Which is why I have no plans to tell her."

"What?" I asked, unable to control the hurt and anger I felt.

"You're out of your mind if you think I'm telling my mother about this."

"So, what? I'm just supposed to be your dirty little secret? Because that's not really my style."

"That's not what I meant, Liv. This isn't about you. It's about my relationship with her. The less my mother knows about my life, especially the people I sleep with, the better we get along."

I understood, of course. There was no way her mother would be accepting of this development. What did I expect her to do? Hand Gail a pamphlet for PFLAG? Still, it bothered me.

"Meanwhile I hide out in the closet, letting her hate me for no reason?"

"You think she'll hate you less if she finds out that we fucked?"

I was no prude, and I certainly didn't mind hearing a bit of spicy talk from the women I slept with. But something about her referring to what we'd just shared in such rough terms bothered me. I guess I'd thought it meant more than a quick fuck, and I hated to think I'd invested more in the experience than she had.

Upset and more than a little angry, I got out of bed and started dressing. I tried to act casual about it, like it was perfectly normal for me to have sex and then saunter off to my apartment (which it was, of course, but that was after meaningless sex— meaningless to both parties). The last thing I wanted was for her to know how much she'd hurt me. Again. "It's late. I should go."

"You don't have to," she said. She looked so disappointed.

"What would Cassie think if I was still here in the morning? What would you tell her?" I asked, unable to keep the anguish out of my voice.

"I'd tell Cassie the truth." She reached for my hand, trying to comfort me.

"And what is the truth?"

"That we're…growing close."

"You can't even tell yourself the truth. You probably should spare your thirteen-year-old daughter the unseemly details."

Before she had a chance to say anything more, I stormed out, leaving both of us to wonder what the hell had gone wrong.

CHAPTER EIGHTEEN

"This is never going to work, Patsy." I barged into her apartment uninvited and flopped onto her couch.

I had been stewing about my fight with Mira almost nonstop since it happened. I still couldn't think about what she'd said the night before without fuming, so I'd avoided her since our argument. Not that she made that easy, at least not initially—five calls in rapid succession (all of which I'd ignored) culminated in one irate message.

"What the hell was that, Liv? I don't even understand what just happened, but I can't ask because the person who knows what went wrong won't speak to me. Obviously we need to talk, so when you're done behaving like a child, call me."

That was the last I'd heard from her, and since I hadn't even expected that much (what did she have to be mad about?), her ire only made me angrier. So far commitment sucked.

As soon as I left work, I headed for Patsy's, seeking commiseration and some guidance, although her relationship expertise pretty much mirrored my own. She didn't seem surprised to see me, which only made me feel more justified in my anger, like Patsy had known from the start that Mira would do something wrong, a promise she had definitely lived up to.

"I assume you're referring to you and Mira," she said, and I nodded. "Why not?"

"For one thing, she's got a kid." I'm not sure where that came from. Aside from me being hyper-aware of Cassie's presence at some inopportune moments, I'd never felt anything but love and admiration for her.

"Who is the only reason you gave Mira a second chance. You adore the kid. The kid is not a problem. Next." As usual, she had no tolerance for my prevarication.

"I wasn't saying Cassie's a problem."

She stared at me blankly, obviously not reading my mind.

"It's just weird to have to…"

"Keep your hormones in check?"

"Yes!"

"Sounds like it's working fine, Liv."

Even if I couldn't tell by the tone of her voice, I knew she was growing impatient with me. Her signature "I've had enough of your foolishness" glare sent the message clearly. One eyebrow raised, lips pursed and frowning, she sighed and crossed her arms over her chest. One of her lectures was obviously ready for takeoff, so I prepared myself for a dressing-down as best I could. Still, I wasn't even close to ready to hear what she had to say.

"You're doing it again."

"Doing what?"

"Squirming your way out of possible happiness."

"I don't know what you're talking about."

"This is what you do. Any time you have more than three dates with a woman you start scrambling for the exit. If you can't find a flaw in her, even something trivial, you invent some other reason for moving on."

I started to protest that it wasn't that bad, but I realized my entire track record with women was a testament to her claim.

Apparently she knew she had me. She smirked and continued as if I'd never opened my mouth. "But this time it's not so easy.

You finally met someone worth your time, someone who could be Mrs. Ollie."

I glowered at her. "What gives you that ludicrous idea?"

"I've known you for twenty years, Liv. You're not as mysterious as you think. You're an open, goddamn frustrating book." She sighed again and settled on the couch next to me. "How often do you come to me for help?"

"Always," I admitted.

"And in the past, how many times have you come to me at the end of one of your flings?"

Never. I just moved from one woman to the next with no more consideration than if I were changing socks. She usually didn't find out that one affair had ended until the next one had begun. Sometimes I was two or three women down the road before she knew I was seeing someone new. That information usually just wasn't important enough to share.

"Something's different this time," she said. "I think it might be something good."

"Are you actually encouraging my relationship with Mira?"

"You've changed, for the better, since you've been spending time with her. Except for today, I haven't seen you this happy since…I've never seen you this happy. I can't believe I'm about to say this, but Mira's good for you."

I let that sink in for a while before I inched closer to the real problem.

"What if she hurts me? What am I saying? She already hurt me. What if she does it again?"

"That doesn't count."

"You were there for the aftermath. You helped me pick up the pieces after she destroyed my life. How can you, of all people, say it doesn't count?"

"Because you weren't in a relationship with her then. She's since apologized. Sincerely. And you forgave her, again before the romance began. She's not the same nineteen-year-old girl who did that, and you're not the same girl she did it to. Give her a chance to show you she's changed and give yourself a chance to be happy."

"She's in the closet, Patsy," I said and filled her in on the details of my fight with Mira.

"Can you blame her?"

"Yes." My indignation withered in the face of her reproving glance.

"This is her first lesbian experience."

"So what?"

"I know you came out in your infancy without any backlash, but your mother wasn't a narrow-minded, homophobic terrorist."

"Fine. She's got good reason to hide this from her mother. Does that mean I have to climb back in the closet with her?"

"No, but you don't have to rip the doors off the hinges either." She was right, of course, and I couldn't believe I'd needed her to point out my transgression. Suddenly, my righteous anger vanished, and I felt despicable. "Maybe you could try being understanding. Have a little patience."

"For how long?"

"You do understand how patience works, don't you?"

"Yes," I said. "I hope Mira does, too."

About an hour after I left Patsy's, I walked up to Mira's front door and rang the bell. I would have been there much sooner, but I had an important stop to make before I could face her again. An eternity passed before the door opened, and as I stood in the glow of her porch light, the cold wind buffeting my face, the air crisp and smelling of snow, I fidgeted with the packets in my hand. They rattled a bit as I shook and rearranged them, trying to decide on the best presentation. I still hadn't figured that out when the door opened, and I shoved them back in my pocket.

Mira seemed surprised to see me there. I guess she hadn't expected me to show up tonight. She wore a ratty old sweatshirt, yoga pants and no makeup, and she looked tired. Her eyes were puffy, and wisps of hair escaped from a haphazard ponytail. I'd never seen her look so disheveled, and I felt even worse for causing her distress.

"I'm sorry," I said. I hoped she would invite me in so we could talk, but if necessary I would say all I had to say there on her front porch. If she decided not to let me back in... Well, I couldn't think about that. "I shouldn't have run out last night or ignored you today, and I really shouldn't have gotten mad at you. It's not up to me who you tell about us or even if you ever tell anyone."

I paused to gather courage, and when I looked at her, I almost chickened out. She looked sad, and I thought that might mean the end for me, for us. But I couldn't leave before I said everything.

"I've slept with a lot of women, but I've never felt so... happy and satisfied after sex as I did last night, and I mean more than physically. I'm just so crazy about you, and the thought that maybe you didn't feel the same, and that you wanted to hide this because you were ashamed of the best thing that's ever happened to me...Well, I couldn't handle that. So I got mad at you for something I had no right to get mad about. I'm sorry," I said again and reached into my pocket for my peace offering. "I've never done this before, but I read somewhere that flowers are customary tools for groveling." I placed the packets in her hand.

Her brow furrowed, and she tilted her head, squinting at the array in obvious confusion.

"I really believe you haven't done this before, Liv. These aren't flowers. These are seeds."

"They're future flowers, and I want to be here, with you, when they bloom. If you'll have me."

I risked another glance at her face, and though her eyes glistened with tears, she was smiling. She kissed me then, a sweet, gentle kiss right there on her front porch for all her neighbors to see.

"I'm not ashamed, Liv, and I'm sorry, too, sorry that I hurt you," she said and invited me in. "Have you eaten? Can you stay for dinner?" She seemed almost shy to ask, as if I could possibly say no.

"I'll stay as long as you want me here," I said and pulled her into an embrace that I never wanted to end.

But then Cassie breezed into the living room, oblivious to the fact that we'd been hugging and that we had abruptly jumped away from each other.

She signed a cursory greeting to me, taking little more interest in my unscheduled presence in her home than she would a chair. "Is the pizza here?" she asked her mother.

"It will be soon," she answered, and I stared at her in disbelief. "Will you set the table, please? For three."

"Can Liv help me?" I knew Cassie loved me, so I took no offense to her opportunistic enthusiasm about me.

"Liv and I need to talk."

"Fine," she signed, and looking put upon as only a thirteen-year-old girl faced with one of her regular household chores can, she moped in the direction of the dining room.

"Pizza? You eat pizza?"

"Are you seriously objecting to junk food?"

"No, I'm just surprised." In all the time since I'd become a regular at her dinner table, she'd always cooked, usually something healthy. I had no idea she ever indulged in the garbage that made up the bulk of my dietary staples.

"It's easy comfort food," she explained. "I didn't feel like cooking."

"So I'm corrupting you in all kinds of ways."

"Most of them good," she said and leaned against me, resting her head on my shoulder. I wrapped my arms around her and kissed the top of her head.

"Still, I'm awfully sorry that I drove you to unhealthy eating."

"And I'm sorry I drove you away." She looked at me intently for a moment before she continued. "I don't really know what I'm doing, but I know that it's right. I want this as much as you do." As if to prove her point, she kissed me—a long, slow, deep kiss, full of promise. I could have lost myself in it for days. "Let's quit apologizing and move on."

That night we made love—an appropriate term for the first time in my life. The tenderness we shared, unlike anything

I'd experienced before, made my heart swell in almost painful bliss. In the moments before I drifted off to sleep in the early hours of the morning, I held her in my arms and listened to her breathing. Her soft skin pressed against mine, warmth radiating from her. I kissed her shoulder and tightened my arms around her. Then I smiled, grateful she'd given me a second chance and that I hadn't deprived myself of any more nights like this.

CHAPTER NINETEEN

If Cassie thought it weird to have me lurking around the breakfast table, she didn't let on. She just sat there reading a book and eating her oatmeal, like I imagined she did every morning. I wasn't sure what to make of that, but I hoped it was a good thing. I had no clue if thirteen was old enough to understand the romantic significance of an extra adult waking up at her house, or if she thought Mira and I had had a sleepover like the one she'd gone to just a few days earlier.

Mira squeezed my shoulder as she shuffled past on her way to the kitchen. She looked adorably sleepy in her terrycloth robe (not traditionally sexy attire, but it was working for me) as she yawned and rubbed her eyes.

"Coffee?" She gestured to the full pot on the counter, and I wrinkled my nose in distaste.

I was certainly tired enough to try choking down a cup, but it was a blissful, achy muscle, contented kind of tired I wanted to savor and enjoy.

"You don't drink coffee? How do you wake up? Please don't tell me you drink pop in the morning."

"Tea."

She stared at me in disbelief, as if I'd asked her to spank me while I called her Mommy.

"Who's the healthy one now?" I teased, and she rolled her eyes, clearly unimpressed by the one healthy choice I'd made in my life.

"I don't have any tea," she apologized.

"I'm fine. I kind of like being tired this morning." I winked, and her wicked grin made me shudder.

Meanwhile Cassie kept her head down, reading her book, seemingly oblivious to our antics. She barely tore her eyes away from the pages of her book to tell me goodbye. Mira, on the other hand, followed me to the door, pouting the whole way.

We both looked back to see if Cassie's book still held her full attention, and then, assured that we weren't about to turn her world upside down, we kissed, the kind of kiss that made me want to head back to Mira's bedroom rather than out the door to work. I almost opened her robe to give my hands better access to her. My fingers hovered over the loose knot at her navel, but I stopped myself. Nothing that happened with her robe undone would make me any more eager to leave.

"I wish you didn't have to go." She rested her forehead against mine and laced our fingers together.

"You're not the only one." I sighed and took a half step away from her. "But I'll see you tonight." I leaned in for a quick kiss on the cheek and then hurried out the door, fearing that if I didn't leave then, I never would.

As it was, I stayed longer than I should have and ended up arriving at the aquarium exactly when I should have been punching in. Any other day I would have been frazzled by my brush with tardiness, but the part of me that normally worried about such things, especially when I hoped to soon be angling for a promotion, was preoccupied by thoughts of Mira. That condition was exacerbated by the fact that I smelled like her— an oddly comforting and distracting consequence of using her shampoo and soap that morning.

Fortunately, my preoccupation wasn't too much of an issue. All of my animals were healthy and thriving, and I moved through the normal activities of my day—morning rounds, food preparation, water testing, all of it—with an oddly conflicting sense of angst and appreciation. Since starting at the aquarium, I'd never dreaded or resented being at work. I loved my job. But that day, I spent a good portion of my shift alternately enjoying the challenges and rewards of my position and wishing I could be with Mira instead.

Nevertheless, even though work was the thing keeping me away from her (even my thoughts during tasks that required more intense focus from me), it was also the reason I'd reconnected with her. If not for this job, for me loving my work so much that I wanted to share that excitement with others, I might never have run into her, or if I had, it might have been without Cassie's conciliatory influence. And now that I had them, I hated to think what my life would be without them.

When I finally sat down, I checked the aquarium's job postings to see if the new position had been added. I checked every day (and had since I first read Roman's unofficial announcement) and gritted my teeth just a little harder each time it wasn't there. The waiting was agony. I didn't know why Roman had decided to torment me with so much advance notice unless he enjoyed the thought of giving me an ulcer. I almost wished he'd never said anything about it, but having known about the job for so many days now, I was ready to submit my updated resume as soon as the posting appeared. That was today.

In all the time I had dreamt of an opportunity like this and waited for the chance to apply, I had envisioned myself submitting the perfect application materials within seconds of the official job posting. I wanted this more than I had ever wanted anything professionally, yet it took several minutes for the reality of it to sink in. I wasn't worried about the job. I thought my chances were good, and even if I didn't get it, I would continue doing work I loved to do. It was an exciting possibility, a fact that didn't change no matter how many times I reread the job description to convince myself I wasn't hallucinating. When I finally clicked *Submit* on my application, my first thought was, "I can't wait to tell Mira." How strange that a long-awaited development at work—an area of my life that was already close to perfect—seemed even better thanks to never-expected developments in my love life, an area I hadn't suspected needed any improvement.

Later that afternoon, feeling like life couldn't possibly get any better, I headed to Mira's house for my first Cassie-sitting session of the week. I thought I'd tell her about the possible promotion (she'd be as excited as I was), but her quizzical expression when she saw me unnerved me. She obviously had something on her mind. I hoped something happened at school that she wanted to talk about, but the possibility that we were headed for a more dreaded personal conversation loomed in my mind. I hated lying to kids, especially ones I admired. Normally I didn't mind sharing with Cassie, but now that the personal details of my life were also, in part, the personal details of her mother's life, I felt less comfortable divulging that information.

"Why were you here this morning?"

This was really not the talk I wanted to have with her. Why couldn't she just need help with her homework?

"Your mom and I were working on something, and by the time we finished what we were doing, it was late, so I slept here."

She didn't just look unconvinced by my half-truth. She looked disappointed. She had clearly expected more from me, and I didn't know how I'd get through this conversation without inspiring that look again. It was not one I enjoyed.

"Are you dating my mom?" she asked after zero lead-up, like she was a Q and A assassin.

My first thought was that, apparently, thirteen *was* old enough to understand adult relationships, at least in part. And though I really thought she should talk to her mother about this, I felt I had to tell her something.

"Would it bother you if I was?"

"No. You're nice to Mom. She seems happy." She looked thoughtful for a minute, and I released the breath I didn't realize I'd been holding. "Grandma Gail will have a stroke," she added.

"We're trying to keep it quiet for now," I told her, and she nodded her understanding.

"Do you love her?" Again with the abrupt, unexpected questions.

"It's a little early to answer that," I told her and felt like I'd avoided the truth again. A more honest answer might have been, "If I could ever love anyone, it would be your mom," but that wasn't completely true either. I already knew what I felt but wasn't ready to admit it.

"That's fair," she signed.

"You are going to talk to your mom about this, right?"

She smiled and nodded. Then after her customary hug, which I appreciated more than usual, she asked if I knew that some jellyfish can eat ten times their body weight in a day.

"And did you know that jellies aren't even fish?"

Our relationship back to normal, she smiled and went off to do her homework. I sent Mira a quick text to let her know about my conversation with Cassie.

Your daughter just grilled me about our relationship. I hope I didn't say too much.

What did you say? Her immediate response made me a little nervous, like I'd get in trouble for saying anything.

Not much. I avoided the question when she asked if we were dating. And if I love you, I neglected to add.

That I can believe. She softened her criticism with a smiley face. *I wonder what made her ask.*

She's intensely observant and too smart for her own good, I replied. *And I hope it's not every day that her mother gropes another woman at the breakfast table.*

That was hardly me groping you, and you know it.

I did know it, and my face flushed to think about it. But it would be torment to consider for too long. Thanks to the longer holiday hours at her store, Mira wouldn't be home until late, possibly after eleven. As far as I was concerned that meant I was definitely spending the night—even if there was only an hour between her return home and my departure for work , I wanted to spend it loving her.

I'll talk to her soon. I promise.
For the record, she thinks I'm good for you, I told her.
Well, she is really smart.

That she was, and I hoped she was also right.

I spent the two hours after Cassie went to bed trying to distract myself by reading, watching television, texting Patsy, doing anything that would keep my mind off Mira. Nothing worked. When she finally walked in the door just before eleven, she didn't even have time to remove her coat before I kissed her. I cupped her face and stroked her delicate cheeks as our lips parted. I pressed her against the door at her back, and she grabbed the front of my shirt in her fist, pulling me closer. Considering the amount of making out we did in her entryway, it was fast becoming one of my favorite places in her house.

"You missed me?" she asked when I finally let us up for air.

"A little, especially since Cassie went to bed and left me all alone," I admitted.

"Was there any more discussion of us?"

"No. She's waiting to talk to you."

"Speaking of which…"

I helped her out of her coat and watched her walk away, appreciating the view. I don't know if I'd failed to notice in the past or if she'd recently cranked up the sex appeal in her wardrobe, but her cleavage-baring top and the black skirt that fell just above her knees definitely caught my attention. I knew I couldn't be the only one who noticed, but I was the only one who could do more than look, a thought that made me smile.

I smiled, too, thinking of what she would tell Cassie and how she would respond. I didn't think Cassie's easy acceptance had been an act, and it pleased me to know that Mira's initial coming out would be so well received. Chances were good that wouldn't always be the case. However, she returned far too soon to have said anything of substance to Cassie. I understood, of course, that it was late and a school night. Cassie needed her rest, and Mira wouldn't be likely to wake her, even for an important discussion.

"She's out of it. She didn't even know I was there." Mira sat in my lap, and the bold familiarity of that act, not to mention her closeness, made my stomach flip.

"It's late," I said and tried not to kiss her right away. We used to talk all the time, and I didn't want her to think I only cared about sex, though I really liked that part of our relationship.

"And it was a long day," she said and leaned against me. It seemed a gesture born not of desire but a need for comfort, so with one hand I gently massaged her shoulders and neck, and was rewarded with a soft "Mmm."

"A rough one?" My other hand (on its own, I swear) started drawing lazy circles on her bare knee, then inching higher.

"It's getting better."

Without even thinking, I began nuzzling her neck and throat while my hand continued its tantalizingly slow journey up her inner thigh. Her hands moved through my hair, and she emitted a satisfied little moan before she pulled away.

"Wait," she said. "I have to ask you something."

"I'm listening." I ran my tongue from her collarbone, along her neck and to her earlobe.

"No, you're not."

"Okay, I'm not, but do you really want me to stop?"

She didn't answer right away, and I resumed my exploration of the soft skin of her throat. My hand drew closer to its destination, and just as I reached the top of her thigh, my fingers grazing her panties, she stopped me.

"This is important," she said.

"Fine." I removed my hands from her body and folded them in front of me. "I promise to be good. I'll keep my hands to myself."

"And your lips."

"And my lips. I'll focus on whatever you have to ask me instead of thinking about your wonderful mouth or your amazing legs or how beautiful you are and how lucky I am."

The impact of her "You're impossible" look was somewhat diminished by an underlying smile.

"What's on your mind?" I asked.

"So." She seemed nervous about saying whatever she had to say. She'd crossed her arms over her abdomen, effectively hugging herself, and was fidgeting a little. I probably should have been nice and helped her out a bit, but she was so cute when she was anxious. I enjoyed watching her squirm. "Christmas is coming up."

"It is."

"Does it bother you?"

"Am I so grumpy that you'd think Christmas bothers me?"

"I mean that you're alone."

"Oh," I said and allowed a little self-pity to creep in. "It did at first, but I got used to it. I usually work, so it's easy to distract myself."

"Are you working this year?"

"I should be. Even when it's my day off, I usually volunteer to take someone else's shift. There's no reason they should miss out on the big family holiday while I sit in my apartment by myself keeping my dust bunnies company. But my boss made me take both days off this year. He says I've worked everyone's fair share of holidays and deserve to have at least one Christmas to myself. So I'll be by myself."

"What if you had another option?" My expression must have conveyed my confusion clearly because she explained before I asked. "You could join Cassie and me."

"What about your mother?"

"She's leaving for Europe on Christmas Eve, so it's just Cassie and me this year, and we both think it would be nice to share the holiday with you." She grabbed my hand excitedly and didn't let go, even after she finished speaking. "You can spend the night and do the whole crack of dawn Santa Claus thing. Or you could come over later if that's too corny for you."

"Really?" I couldn't believe they would want me to be a part of their Christmas, that they would open their home to me like that.

"Of course," Mira answered. She squeezed my hand but seemed almost shy, as if she was afraid I'd say no. But honestly, how could I?

"I'd love to. Thank you."

"Now where were we?" she asked and grinned that wicked grin she'd flashed that morning.

In a good place, I thought in the half second before her lips were on mine. A really good place.

CHAPTER TWENTY

Of course it couldn't be that simple just to slide into some sort of Christmas-inspired domestic bliss. Certainly it was sweet of Mira to again include me in her family's holiday plans, even sweeter that she was nervous to ask me, as if I'd say no to anything she requested—with the probable exception of being friendly to her mother.

But in addition to my first real Christmas celebration in close to two decades, I'd also acquired a new and unfortunate familiarity with the stress so many feel around the holidays. I mean, really, in the past fifteen years, my gift-giving experience had been limited to Patsy's rather forgiving and unconventional attitude toward presents. One year I gave her a gross of condoms, and she thanked me more genuinely than when I bought her the purse she'd dropped SUV-sized hints about wanting.

"I won't have to buy condoms for at least three months," she'd exclaimed before declaring it the Best Christmas Ever.

But giving a present to someone I was sleeping with? That had never happened, in large part thanks to the brevity and well-timed endings of all my previous affairs. Better yet, this wasn't just someone I was sleeping with. It was Mira, and this wasn't just any Christmas gift. It was for the woman who'd made me reexamine my whole view of dating, on our first Christmas together. And the fact that I anticipated future holidays with her without slipping into hysteria at the thought meant this present was a big deal, one of those make or break moments. This would set the tone for all future holidays and special occasions. Too understated and she would get the impression I didn't care enough or wasn't invested in our relationship. But if I went to an extravagant extreme so early on, I would set the bar too high and probably come off as needy, clingy or possibly creepy.

So after careful consideration I was left with little more to go on than that I should avoid jewelry (too much, too soon, even if I could afford it) and lingerie (somewhat distasteful and more of a gift for me than for her).

When I asked her for guidance (in what I hoped was a nonchalant and not too obviously panicked way), she offered no help.

"Oh I don't need anything," she replied sweetly (not really answering the question of what she *wanted*). "I'm just happy you'll be here."

Uh-huh.

"Does that mean you want me for Christmas?"

"I always want you," she said, inspiring a pleasant tightening of my stomach. "And it could be fun to unwrap you." She winked, and my stomach was no longer alone in its response to her.

"I'll be sure to wear a bow," I managed to say before our communication switched to non-verbal.

Playful banter aside, I was still fretting over her Christmas present. I might have been new to this whole relationship thing, but I was learning to speak Girlfriend. I translated her "I don't need anything" comment fairly easily: not only did she want a gift, but she also expected something thoughtful. More importantly, I was on my own.

I almost wished I was still alone and my biggest holiday concern whether I'd find someone amusing to pass Christmas night with or if I'd be left with old movies as entertainment. But the prospect of waking up on Christmas morning snuggled in Mira's comfy bed, holding her in my arms before gathering with her and Cassie by a cozy fire and a pile of presents under a glowing tree seemed so much better than waking up alone in my bleak and lonely apartment, no matter how nerve-wracking the lead-up. It put all of my ridiculous worrying into perspective. I'd figure something out, and I had decent odds of not screwing it up.

Meanwhile, life outside of agonizing over Christmas presents kept rolling along, bringing its own stress and complications with it.

At the top of my Things Not About Mira and Me list of issues was the promotion at work. I'd heard absolutely nothing since I got the automated email confirming receipt of my application. The aquarium had generously given employees until after the holidays to submit their resumes. Really, though, if anyone needed that much time to pull everything together and apply, they probably weren't cut out for a job that would require a certain amount of organization and preparedness, or so I told myself. Because my competitors had, in theory, not yet all been amassed in some official file somewhere and wouldn't be until the new year began, I wouldn't hear anything until at least the middle of January, but the agonizing interval between putting in for the job and getting any news tested my already limited patience in that area.

"You know you're being silly, right?" Mira said one afternoon as I absent-mindedly helped her hang Christmas lights on her house. She claimed she typically tended to that task right after Thanksgiving but that this year she had been somewhat distracted. "This job is perfect for you. And you for it."

"I think so," I said. "I just hope Roman and the board see it that way."

I steadied the ladder as she reached farther than I liked. Even though I'd never decorated anything for any holiday except the occasional jack-o-lantern at Halloween, I tried to convince her to let me do the scary climbing. I really would have preferred to be the one breaking my neck by tumbling from her roof or the ladder, but she unequivocally refused. Given my lack of focus, I was better off on the ground, but I still held my breath every time she exhibited too much confidence in her aerial skills.

"I've done this all by myself every year for the last ten years, usually while also keeping an eye on Cassie. You don't have to worry. About me or the job."

"That really puts my mind at ease," I said, certain she picked up on the sarcasm.

"You know my daughter?"

"Cute girl, kind of intense?"

"That's the one."

She looped the strand of lights around one of the small hooks near the gutter. I briefly wondered if she'd installed the hooks herself, and a flash of super-feminine, skirt and heel wearing Mira wielding power tools in her determination to make Christmas happen flashed in my mind. Another distraction I didn't need when my girlfriend was on the verge of a trust fall from several feet off the ground.

"She raved about your class for weeks—a class you not only taught but invented. And she wasn't the only one who loved it. I heard other students and their parents talking about what a great experience it was. I'm sure whoever makes the decision about this job knows what a success it was and what an asset you are. You've already proven you can do the job, so quit tormenting yourself."

Much to my relief, she stepped off the ladder and onto solid ground just as the wind picked up, whipping her hair across her face. She reached to restrain it at the same time as I moved to brush it away. Her ruddy cheeks felt cold, and I stroked them gently with my thumbs.

"We can go shopping if you want, buy some clothes for the interview I'm sure you're going to have. It might help you feel better about this."

"How would that help exactly? Retail therapy has never proven useful in my case."

"Because you'll shift your focus to getting this job rather than convincing yourself that it will never happen."

"Interesting theory," I said, pondering the potential merits of being optimistically proactive. Even if the thought of shopping with Mira didn't call to mind the other area of great stress in my life (namely shopping *for* Mira), I doubted I'd opt for one of my least favorite activities, no matter what the chances it would put my mind at ease. "I'll get back to you."

One corner of her mouth curved upward, but she said nothing. Instead she plugged in the lights, and we stepped back to admire the transformation. I couldn't help but smile at how exorbitantly cheery her home looked with the multi-colored lights glowing along the eaves and porch railings, around the windows and in her bushes. She had warned me that she tended to go overboard for Christmas, and now that the outside of her house rivaled downtown Chicago as a source of light pollution, I believed her. Her next focus would be the Christmas tree—a real tree that she wanted me to help her and Cassie pick out and decorate.

My inner conservationist cringed at the excess of it all, but I managed to say nothing. And as we stood together on her front lawn, bathed in the artificial light of a thousand colored bulbs, she sighed contentedly, wrapped her arm around my waist and rested her head on my shoulder. Environment be damned, I would have stayed there staring at the surfeit of holiday joy until June just to keep her happy.

"There's no way Santa will miss your house," I said.

"Oh, he never does. He loves it here." She took my hand, and we walked back toward her gleaming home, ready to pack up her decorating supplies and go inside. "You really don't need to worry about the job," she said, already knowing me well enough to understand that, no matter how unruffled I might appear, inside I had succumbed to anxiety. She gave my hand a gentle squeeze. "I know without a doubt that you'll get it, but if for some bizarre reason you don't, you still have Cassie and me as consolation prizes, and we adore you." She pulled me in for a hug, one of those surprisingly strong embraces that somehow makes everything better. "I think you're the smartest woman I know and the greatest teacher Cassie has ever learned from. You're stuck with us. For a long, long time."

Then she kissed me, a soft, reassuring peck that made my heart swell and flutter. Just knowing she believed in me so fervently made an enormous difference. For so long I'd had no one other than Patsy in my corner, and now, with Mira and, to a degree, Cassie, I'd more than doubled my support system. That feeling of comfort and emotional reinforcement was more than mutual, and I wished Mira could know how readily I would be there to support her, under any circumstance. In that moment, I realized exactly what I should get her for Christmas, and I actually became excited about joining the herds of holiday shoppers doing their best to single-handedly save the economy.

Of course, our giant admiration and encouragement fest led to another issue—what I called The Friends Conundrum. I spent every possible second with Mira. I hadn't slept in my own bed since she'd forgiven me for being an ass about coming out, and I didn't return to my apartment for days at a time because, with the exception of a fresh change of clothes, there was nothing there I needed. Unfortunately, my neglect didn't limit itself to the tiny corner of the world I called my home. Aside from semi-regular texts and a brief phone call or two, I'd abandoned Patsy as well.

I think I liked you better when you were whoring around, she texted after a week and a half of sporadic contact. *At least trampy Liv was available between sexual partners.*

Ouch. Patsy, never one to waste time on subtleties, had no trouble telling me exactly when and how I screwed up. Most of the time I was smart enough to fix the problem right away.

"I guess I had that coming," I said when she answered her phone. This conversation seemed too important to leave to the potential misinterpretation and bewilderment of texting.

"Of course you did." I could picture the aggravated expression she must have worn in that moment.

"I'm sorry I disappeared. I was working so hard at being a good girlfriend that I forgot to be a good friend, and that's not okay."

"No, Ollie, it's not."

I winced at the Ollie. For us, that was the best friend equivalent of a mother using her child's full name. However, the inherent friendliness of the nickname she'd assigned me in college (even though I'd come to hate it) gave me hope that I hadn't gone too far this time. Had she called me Olivia (something that hadn't happened in close to twenty years), I would have been ready to admit defeat. Still, she obviously wouldn't be forgiving me easily or soon.

Not that I deserved much leniency. She showed an insane amount of loyalty to her friends. It wasn't much to ask not to be abandoned when reciprocal devotion became something of a challenge. It wasn't like she had all the time in the world to lavish on her friends. She worked hard at a time-consuming job, and she had a big family that she loved, including several nieces and nephews and godchildren, all of whom adored her and loved spending time with her. Nevertheless, she always made time for me, and I couldn't blame her for feeling angry that I, with my near total lack of interpersonal obligations, hadn't shown her the same respect.

"I'm sorry," I said again. "I'm all yours now. If you're available and hungry, I'll buy you dinner tonight, but I understand if you're busy."

"What if I'm not interested?"

Ouch again. "Then I'll have to come up with a better offer."

She took a century to respond, and I started worrying in earnest that I had really botched things this time.

"Does dinner include drinks?" she finally asked.

"I'm still me."

"All right. But I get to pick where we eat."

I wouldn't have it any other way, I thought as we settled on a time and place to meet. I hung up feeling hopeful I could remind her why she loved me even when I didn't deserve it.

When I called Mira to break the bad news of my absence that evening to her, she revealed a similar issue on her side. Megan, Sarah and Tiffany (who seemed incapable of acting as individuals) had been pestering her since she fell off the face of the earth some time in the middle of fall. Thinking back, I hadn't heard her mention her personal pack of opportunistic hyenas in months, and though I hadn't missed the sycophantic trio (not even the thought of them), they were still her friends. Apparently she saw some redeeming qualities in them, and I understood she needed to spend time with them soon.

"The girls want to get together this weekend. Cassie will be at her grandparents' house for their early Christmas celebration, and I'm miraculously not working the Saturday night before Christmas. It seems like as good a time as any. What do you think?"

She sounded tentative and anything but enthusiastic, like she was afraid I'd try to discourage her from seeing her friends. True, I was disappointed that part of our adults only weekend was being commandeered, but I wanted her to be happy. If time with Megan, Sarah and Tiffany somehow managed to produce happiness, I wouldn't stand in the way.

"That's fine," I said, trying to sound enthusiastic about it. "I'll see if Patsy's free to entertain me, assuming she forgives me."

"Oh, I thought—never mind."

"Tell me."

"Well, they're sure I've been too busy for them because of the new man in my life, which is sort of true. I couldn't exactly deny it, so they wouldn't let it go. I finally admitted that I'm seeing someone just to shut them up."

"Okay." I had a terrible feeling about what was coming.

"And now they want us all to go out on Saturday, *all* of us, meaning you're invited."

"Really?" I felt like I must be missing something. There was no way those three would blithely accept me as Mira's girlfriend and joyfully welcome me into the fold.

"They, uh," she cleared her throat, "they want to meet the reason they haven't seen me."

There it was. "And you didn't tell them they already have, did you?"

"Not exactly."

A surprise outing. This would be great.

"So they have no idea what they're about to walk into," I said.

"No, but I want to tell them about us. I just...I'll feel better if you're with me, braver I guess."

Well, that did it. If Mira needed me there, how could I say anything but yes?

"I'm in," I said.

"Really? You're okay with this? I know they aren't your favorite people."

"Honey, I'd do just about anything if it means I get to spend the night with you instead of just wishing I was. Don't you know that?"

"I do now." I swore I could hear her smiling, and I knew I was grinning like an idiot as she told me to have fun—but not too much fun—with Patsy and to hurry back to her when I was done.

"And Liv," she said just before I hung up. "I like when you call me honey."

"Me too."

CHAPTER TWENTY-ONE

Not surprisingly, Patsy's choice for her forgiveness dinner landed us not at an actual restaurant but at Red's, a bar that happened to serve food—a textbook Patsy choice. Not that she didn't care about what she ate. She just cared about what she drank more. The bar's décor fell somewhere between Irish pub and rustic: kind of sticky with lots of wood paneling and "authentic" Irish artifacts adorning the walls. Mostly this consisted of ads for Guinness and shamrocks in various sizes and media—stained glass, ceramic, rusty tin and a few tattered paper cutouts left over from St. Patrick's Day.

The bar owners had also upped their legitimacy by inscribing the bathroom doors with the Irish words "Fir" and "Mná" instead of (not in addition to) "Men" and "Women." The only other indication of which restroom was which was the presence of urinals in the Fir room, which I discovered on my first trip to the bathroom. It wasn't the first time I ended up in the men's room at a bar, though this was more out of confusion than desperation or drunkenness. Since there were decent odds I'd find an equally confused man in the Mná room if I switched, I stayed put. Toilet confusion aside, I liked the place. On top of welcoming Patsy like she was Norm on *Cheers* (resulting in a substantial discount on our tab), they made a decent cheeseburger, and the beer selection was good. What else did I need?

I spent the first thirty minutes or so of our meal grilling Patsy about her job (she was beyond ready for Christmas break), her family (all healthy with two more babies on the way), her Christmas plans (the usual big family party to which I was, as always, invited) and Alex (still not boring). Pretty much everything was fair game if it helped me avoid talking about Mira, whose prominence in my thoughts had gotten us into this mess to begin with. Perhaps I was a bit overzealous in my efforts to make Patsy the focus of the evening, but I hated that I'd hurt her feelings. I wanted her to know that I hadn't stopped caring about her. Apparently she got the picture.

"Easy, tiger. At this rate you're going to run out of thoughtful questions before dessert. Did I mention you're buying me dessert?"

"As if you needed to."

"You can talk about her, you know. I won't be offended."

"I thought it was a sore subject."

"A little, but I want you to be happy more than I want your undying devotion."

"I could offer you enduring devotion instead," I said.

"I won't settle for anything less than constant," she countered.

"Stop. You're too good to me." I guessed we were in a good place if she was joking about it. Just to be safe, I told her, "I mean it. I really don't deserve you."

"No, you don't, but I've stuck with you this long. I can't quit now." Had either of us been the touchy-feely type, we almost certainly would have hugged in that moment. Instead we both finished our beers and flagged down the waitress for another round. "How are things going?"

"It's weird. It seems like it should be harder, you know?" I said, marveling at how easy it was to be with Mira and Mira alone.

"I do know, and it's totally weird." She pushed a french fry around her plate, smiling to herself. I needed to meet Alex the Miracle Worker soon. "But things are going well?"

"Really well. Maybe too well."

"Meaning?"

"We're going out with her friends on Saturday," I said and explained Mira's plan to tell Tiffany, Megan and Sarah about us.

"She's telling people now?" I nodded, grateful that, thanks to Patsy's wise counsel, I'd given Mira enough space to reach this step. "That's huge. Also terrifying."

I was pretty much dreading my upcoming night out with the girls, and Patsy's comment validated my fears. Unlike me, she'd been almost close to Mira and her lackeys in college. Even though we were a year ahead of them, Patsy, who got along with everyone, welcomed them into her expansive circle of friends. She had found them mildly irritating at first, but credited their immaturity for their annoying behaviors. However, once the rape story started circulating and Patsy learned that irritating and annoying were the best her four youthful acquaintances had to offer, she cut them out without hesitation or remorse, which meant that most of her friends went back to ignoring them as well. It didn't make life as a would-be rapist any easier, but at least I had the satisfaction of seeing them suffer too. That was the moment I first realized how fortunate I was to have Patsy.

"I'm happy she's telling them and that she wants me there, but part of me wishes they'd all get food poisoning and cancel."

"Do I have to ask why?"

"It's mostly not for the reason you think," I said. "I'm not looking forward to spending time with them, but more than that, I'm afraid Mira is going to end up disappointed. I hope I'm wrong, but her friends never struck me as being particularly open-minded. Or supportive. Or sincere. Or human. I think she's expecting them to be surprised but accepting."

"What are you expecting?" She turned her gaze to the worn and stained tent card with the brief list of dessert possibilities.

"At best, I'm going to bite my tongue a lot."

"At worst?" She zeroed in on the apple pie, and I could almost hear the words à la mode rumbling around her brain.

"Mira will do so much crying on my shoulder that I'm going to look like I just crawled out of the lake."

"As long as you're not being dramatic," she said and finished another beer. "Maybe they'll surprise you. It's possible they've changed." Incredulous, I stared at her, waiting for her to recognize the improbability of that scenario. "Okay, it's also possible that it will be ninety-five degrees and sunny on Christmas. My point is that it doesn't help anything to decide they're going to be awful and wait for it to happen. You're there to support Mira, not avenge the wrongs of the past, so maybe you should be a little open-minded yourself."

"You're right." I nodded, appreciating the reminder of why I was willingly stepping through the gates of hell, and for Mira's sake, I could pretend that her friends were decent, likeable people. They might amaze me with their transformation.

But I doubted it.

I managed to drink more with Patsy than I'd intended, a standard pitfall of any time spent with her. I ended up on the far side of tipsy though not exactly drunk, but even with my senses dimmed as they were, I still figured out pretty soon after getting to Mira's house that her mood wasn't entirely joyful.

She stood at the sink finishing up the last of the dinner dishes, and as always, she looked amazing. She wore jeans that must have been made specifically for her and a thin, white T-shirt that hung loosely on her slender frame. Part of me wanted to lean against the wall and watch her, but the larger part of me demanded physical contact.

"I missed you," I said, and she jumped as if she hadn't heard me approach, but she leaned into the hug I gave her from behind. She even moaned a little when I lifted her hair and began nuzzling her neck. She smelled better than usual. I couldn't pinpoint the difference—new shampoo? Different soap? I wasn't sure, but I liked it.

"You smell extra good today," I sighed into her ear before kissing it.

"A customer was trying to decide if he wanted to buy some perfume for his girlfriend, and I got hit in the testing crossfire."

She didn't let go of the plate in her hand, but she seemed to have forgotten about washing it. "We should consider ourselves lucky it was one of the nicer fragrances available."

"I'm counting my blessings," I said and returned my attentions to the delicate skin at the nape of her neck.

"How was your night? Did you have a good time?" She sounded almost nervous, though I couldn't imagine why.

"It was fun. Patsy loves me again." I moved my hands to her waist, running my fingers just under her shirt. I heard a shift in her breathing and smiled against the spot on her neck that had most of my attention.

"So it was just the two of you?"

"Yep," I answered, wondering belatedly if Cassie was safely preoccupied with homework or, even better, already asleep. I knew it was too early for bed, and I didn't really wish her away. I just didn't want her barreling through the kitchen and getting an eyeful.

"No one joined you?"

"Like who?" I asked before shifting my focus to the sensitive spot just below her ear.

"Like Patsy's boyfriend. Or any lesbian in the city who happened to pass by and decide you needed company."

I stopped kissing her then and turned her to face me. "You think I was out picking up other women?"

"No." She shifted her gaze to her festive Santa Claus socks rather than maintaining eye contact. "Maybe."

So much for this being easy, I thought and moved away from her. I leaned against the counter, folded my arms across my chest and tried not to let my anger get the best of me.

"Care to explain?"

"Isn't that what you do with Patsy—drink and pick up women?"

"Most of the time, yes." I probably shouldn't have been so blunt, but she had hurt me with her accusation. How could she possibly think I would cheat on her?

"I know you've been drinking, so…"

"So you assume I somehow forgot that I've already fallen for the sexiest, kindest, most self-sufficient and randomly needy woman on the planet?"

"Well, when you put it like that." She tried to downplay her concerns, but I wasn't ready to brush them aside. I'd never seen her so insecure except when her mother was around, and I did not want to share any similarities with her mother. I thought we needed to talk about what was bothering her, if for no other reason than I didn't like her doubting me.

"I'm not your husband," I told her.

"I'm well aware of that." Looking confused, she moved toward me.

"Then why are you expecting the same behavior from me that you got from him?" Her progress forward stopped like she'd been hit by something. She bit her lips and looked away again, saying nothing.

"We've got a lot working against us here, you know?" I stepped away from her again, needing the distance between us. "There's my history, which doesn't really scream Long-Term Monogamous Relationship Girl. It's pretty much the opposite. And then there's your past. Your husband made a habit of cheating on you. And for the record, not being satisfied with a woman like you makes him just about the stupidest prick on the planet in my book." A bitter little laugh escaped her. "He treated you badly, and I can't imagine his behavior filled you with confidence. I don't blame you for feeling gun-shy, but I need you to trust me, Mira. I'm not like him."

"I want to believe that." She still refused to look at me. If he weren't already dead, I would've killed Cole Morgan for unnerving her so.

"What is it you think another woman could offer me that you don't?"

She shrugged but stayed silent.

"There's nothing I could get from any other woman that I don't already get from you." I moved to her then and gently lifted her face so we made eye contact. "I'm sure there were other women at the bar tonight—there must have been—but

I didn't notice any of them. You're it for me, honey. There's no one else."

The corners of her mouth curved slightly upward, the ghost of a smile, but it didn't reach her eyes or remove the furrow from her brow. Even though it hurt that she doubted me, it hurt more to see her so broken up. I needed to comfort her somehow.

"I don't let a lot of people in. I never have. When I was a kid, it was just me and my mom, and I was happy with that. It was enough. But when she died, that was it. I had Patsy, but otherwise I was alone. It was devastating, but over time I convinced myself that I was fine with it. I wasn't lonely, and I didn't need anybody. It was pretty easy once I forgot what I was missing." She drew in a sharp breath and looked at me with such sadness I almost regretted saying anything. I hadn't brought this up to get pity. It was just the best way I could think of to explain to her how much this relationship meant to me.

"But since you came back into my life, it's been different. It's been better. You and Cassie have filled a place I didn't even know was empty, and I don't want it to be empty again. I couldn't stand it. You're my favorite person in this world. You're my family, and even if it takes you forever to believe me, I'm not going to throw this away for a quickie on the side. I'm not going back to having no family, not for anything."

I could have said more if I'd been just a little bit braver, but I could tell I'd made my point. Though she was on the verge of tears, her grin hinted that they were happy tears.

"You keep doing this to me," she sniffed and swiped the tears from her cheeks. "I'm sorry. I know you aren't like him, and you shouldn't have to remind me."

She hugged me then, and I thought I'd never want to let go. I wasn't naïve enough to believe this would be our last conversation on this topic. She likely would still have to wrestle with the lingering doubts her marriage had burdened her with, but in that instant, everything was right between us. I didn't want the moment to end. Reassured by the solidity of her in my arms, reveling in the smell of her, I felt tears threaten, but I refused to let them fall, even in the face of the most tender, least sexual embrace I'd ever shared with anyone.

I didn't know how long we held onto each other, but eventually our hug ended with a sweet, lingering kiss. When she finally drifted back to the dishes in her sink, I followed.

"How did Cassie get out of dish duty?" I grabbed a towel to help her. "Homework or puppy dog eyes?"

"A bit of both, actually, but mostly homework."

"Does she need any help?"

"Are you clear-headed enough?"

"Depends on the subject," I admitted.

"I think it was the amount of homework, not difficulty, so she should be fine, but we can check on her in a little while."

"Lucky me. That means I get to help you."

"You didn't make any of the dishes. You shouldn't have to do them."

"As much fun as it is to watch you—I mean, really, you even make housework hot—what I'd like better is to make up some more. I had no idea how good that could be."

"What did you have in mind?"

"For now, I thought maybe it would be good for us to watch a movie."

"Really." She seemed doubtful. "What movie?"

"Doesn't matter. I just really like watching movies with you." A slight blush reached her cheeks. "But I know you won't relax and enjoy the, um, movie if the kitchen is still a mess, so…" I reached for a plate in the dish rack, but she blocked me, her hand on my chest.

"I really like watching movies with you, too." She kissed me then, her tongue dancing across my lips before demanding entry. Her hands slid up to my shoulders, pulling me closer, and I grabbed her by the waist, my thumbs slipping under her shirt and skimming the unbelievably soft skin of her abdomen. I was just about to throw her up on the counter, dishes and Cassie be damned, when she bit my lower lip and pulled away. "Movie preview," she whispered, the low timbre of her voice driving me even crazier.

Somehow I managed to focus on the dishes, moving as fast as I could to get us back to the kissing, though first we had to check on Cassie and maybe invite her to watch a movie with us, which meant making out would be on hold a while longer. Really, I didn't care for all these obstacles to the kissing.

We worked silently for several minutes, my racing thoughts alternating between that kiss and the discussion that preceded it. Who would've believed that I would ever get to this place? Not only was I in a real relationship, but instead of running away or losing my temper when things got challenging, I'd managed to channel my inner Patsy and deal with the problem. Stranger still? Evidence that I was in love with Mira Butler, of all people, kept stacking up, and it didn't terrify me.

"So," she interrupted my sappy inner monologue. "I'm your favorite person?"

There was only one way to answer that. "Don't tell Patsy."

CHAPTER TWENTY-TWO

Cassie left with her grandparents on Friday night, and though I had spent the better part of that afternoon getting the inside scoop on Mira's former in-laws while helping Cassie wrap her Christmas presents for them (which was about as helpful as flossing with a jump rope), I made myself scarce before they arrived to avoid any awkward exchanges with Mr. and Mrs. Morgan. Based on what I could hear from my hideaway in Mira's bedroom, they sounded nice enough, but my perception was somewhat clouded by the distance and closed door between us, not to mention my dormant sorrow and anger over ignoring my role in Cassie's life and her importance to mine. I said nothing to Mira after she sprang me from gay prison. She already felt blue about Cassie's absence, and I didn't want to compound her gloomy state with my complaints, but I wondered if I'd ever get to meet Cassie's good grandparents and if they'd ever even know that I existed. Considering the giant step Mira planned to take the following night, I held out hope for a formal meeting with the Morgans someday, preferably before Cassie started college.

Mira worked until early evening on Saturday, so after seeing her off that morning (maybe a little late, but definitely happy), I headed home to putter around my apartment rather than sit alone in her house wishing she or Cassie or both of them were there with me. My few small rooms seemed so tiny and drab after so much time away. I wondered how, with my lack of space and expansive view of the brick exterior of the building next door, I'd ever felt comfortable and not claustrophobic there. And why had I never decorated? I'd been in the apartment close to eight years yet had done almost nothing to personalize it—aside from some refrigerator magnets and one picture of my mom and me. Everything in my place was functional and utilitarian, not at all like the cozy, colorful home where I now spent the majority of my time. My apartment, I realized, was a place to eat, sleep and read, not a place to live.

When I wasn't cataloging the flaws in my up-to-that-point adequate living space, I gave myself a pep talk about seeing The Evil Trio, who, I acknowledged, I needed to start thinking of in less hostile terms, at least until they proved me right. We were meeting for drinks, a near perfect turn of events in my opinion. If ever I could be guaranteed success in a social activity, it was meeting people for drinks. I excelled at drinks. They were a nice, low-pressure get-together, combining the soothing effects of alcohol with lower commitment expectations than dinner. The comfortable familiarity (of the activity at least) had me thinking we might make it through the night unscathed. But should Mira's coming out go the way of the Titanic or the Hindenburg, drinks also offered a far easier escape than being locked into a meal.

And though disaster seemed like a realistic possibility, I reminded myself that Mira, who I now knew was not just a vapid, superficial, airheaded princess, had remained friends with these women for close to twenty years. She knew them far better than I could ever hope (or want) to, so I felt there had to be some good in them for her to cultivate such a lengthy friendship. But if it did go south, well, it would only be a couple of hours of our lives. I'd survived whole months of misery, mostly at the hands of the women I hoped to impress that evening, and none of that time held the promise of intimacy with Mira afterward as a reward.

By the time I left my apartment to meet Mira, I'd achieved a level of calm about the evening's main event, a calm that disappeared as soon as I saw my date. She looked stunning (no surprise there), but the stark contrast between my jeans and sweater and her almost knee-length dress—a dark gray number that showed off her gorgeous legs and displayed the most incredible cleavage I'd ever had the fortune of laying my eyes on—made me feel like I'd worn sweatpants to the prom.

I think I offered a wildly eloquent compliment along the lines of "Wow" before following her back to her bedroom.

"I'm almost ready. Can you zip me the rest of the way up?"

"That goes against every impulse I have right now."

"Try your hardest." She hit me with a look that probably was intended as admonishing but ended up being more seductive.

I inched the zipper lower. "Gravity seems to be working in my favor rather than yours."

"Gravity needs to behave."

"It always does," I told her. "It's law."

"Liv," she said, her voice a gentle rebuke. "We'll be late."

"I'm all right with that," I said.

"I'm not."

She sounded flustered (and not at all like she'd agree that sex before coming out to her friends was a great idea), so I relented and moved the zipper back in the direction she wanted it.

"You're a bad influence."

"Hardly. I am a role model, a mentor."

"Not in this room you aren't."

"Are you sure about that?"

"Yes." Her mouth took possession of mine then, and she kissed me—expertly. Her hands moved through my hair, and her tongue danced with mine as she steered me backward onto the bed. Just as I thought I was about to get my way, she broke the kiss. "Now sit there and behave."

"Yes, ma'am," I said, not minding that my punishment meant watching her decide which pair of heels worked best with her dress. They all looked great to me, but the longer I watched her, the more I felt like the before picture on a makeover show.

"Do I look okay?" It was a question I hadn't asked since I left high school, and to her credit, she picked up on the underlying meaning.

"Are you nervous?"

"Pffft." I waved my hand in the air between us. "It's just drinks with your best friends, who have never liked me, but I'm sure that will change the second they find out I've turned you gay. What's there to be nervous about?"

I fell backward on her bed and blew out an anxious, exasperated breath. She sat beside me and took my hand.

"Don't worry about this. It's going to be fun."

"Easy for you to say. They already love you."

"And they'll love you, too. Just be yourself and they can't not love you. You have that effect on people. Believe me, I know."

"If you say so," I muttered and sat up, wondering how much merit to give to her roundabout admission that she couldn't help but love me. "Do you want me to change?" I asked, tugging at my sweater. "Not that I have a lot of options here, but I'm feeling a little underdressed for the occasion."

"I told you to be yourself. This is you, and you look fantastic." She kissed me, a soft, reassuring peck.

"*You* look fantastic. You always do."

"I like dressing up."

"That is such a foreign concept to me."

"It helps to have such a rapt, appreciative audience. And it doesn't hurt to know that you'll be helping me out of this dress." I moved to oblige, but she caught my hand. "At the *end* of the night."

"Fine." I stood and took her hand, ready to get this over with.

As if I needed another reminder that I was out of my element, the bar we ended up at wasn't a bar at all, at least not according to my exhaustive experience. The proprietors called it a dramshop, and they'd decorated it like some sort of hipster art student's idea of an antique laboratory. If that wasn't enough to further fuel my aversion to this entire evening, the service sealed the deal. I could have lived without the looks of derision when I asked for a beer instead of wine or one of their drams, especially from people who clearly had no idea that *dram* wasn't a synonym for wildly expensive craft cocktail.

Before we got to order drinks, however, we had to get to the table where Tiffany, Megan and Sarah lurked, an eventuality I tried once more to delay.

"Have you considered easing them into this?" I stopped just past the supercilious doorman. "I could check our coats and wait at the bar while you execute Phase One."

"Phase One?" Her eyebrows almost disappeared in her hairline.

"You tell them that your date is a woman. Let them absorb that surprising news, and once they've gotten over their shock, you give me the signal to join you for Phase Two, which is me. I think it's a workable plan." She favored me with my favorite "You're impossible" look, but I pressed on. "I'm thinking of your friends. You want them to survive this, don't you? The gradual approach might be your ally."

"I'm leaning more toward the rip the bandage off approach," she said and grabbed my hand, leading me toward the back of the bar where her friends waited. I had just enough time to lose my panicked expression before my big debut.

"Oh my fucking god," I heard as I rounded a corner behind her. I didn't know who said it—Tiffany, Megan or Sarah—because they all gaped at us, mouths hanging open, eyes locked on Mira's hand in mine.

She moved to hug each of her friends, whether they wanted to or not, and I studied each of their faces as they continued to stare. Sarah regarded us with surprise and wonder, her blue eyes wide and unblinking, her eyebrows arched to what I suspected were their limits. Megan, also obviously taken aback, had neglected to close her mouth after her initial shock. She blinked repeatedly—possibly to correct her vision and unsee the bewildering sight before her. Meanwhile, Tiffany's eyes had narrowed to slits, her thin lips formed a scowl, and her pinched expression held a bit less wonder and a bit more haughty, Gail Butler-like judgment. As I'd expected, they'd all been jolted by Mira's startling revelation. The consternation was plainly written on each of their faces, but the one thing missing—from two-thirds of them anyway—was the hostility I'd expected. Maybe we would withstand this after all.

"Is this a joke?" Tiffany asked.

"What the hell?" Megan said at the same time.

Not to be left out, Sarah offered a simple, "Mira?"

"I told you I started seeing someone new," she said matter-of-factly. She presented our relationship as completely ordinary, which, I understood, was how she expected her friends to take it.

"You couldn't have been more specific?" Megan asked.

And ruin all the fun? I thought but wisely stayed quiet.

"This seemed more like an in-person conversation."

"With visual aids," Sarah said, and I suppressed a laugh. It was early yet, but I already liked Sarah more than I thought possible.

I noticed Tiffany hadn't said anything since Mira confirmed that this was, in fact, not a joke, but the permanent grimace hadn't left her face. The pot-stirrer in me wanted to focus on her, ask her questions, make her acknowledge what she so clearly wanted to deny, but for Mira's sake, I kept myself in check. It helped that, before Mira and I even removed our coats and sat down, a bubbly waitress scuttled up to the table to take our orders.

"How?" Sarah asked as soon as our slightly less effervescent server bounced away to retrieve Mira's wine and my somewhat disappointing (based on her crestfallen expression) beer. To Sarah's credit, she seemed more intrigued than disturbed.

"Voodoo," Tiffany muttered and turned her sour expression on her cocktail. Either Mira didn't hear, or she chose to ignore her friend's comment.

"It was gradual," I offered.

"How long did it take Ollie to wear you down?" Megan asked.

I cleared my throat and shifted uncomfortably in my seat, but Mira placed a calming hand on my thigh, telegraphing the message that she would correct her friends on both mistakes.

"Actually, if I'd left it up to *Liv*," she stressed my name and raised a corrective eyebrow at her friends, "we still wouldn't be here."

"You mean *you*—"

"Seduced Liv," Mira explained to a baffled Megan. "She resisted my advances for quite some time. I had to resort to drastic measures to get her to notice me."

Megan's mouth fell open again, and Tiffany continued to frown at any inanimate object in her line of sight. Sarah, however, nodded her head a few times, as if nudging her understanding into place. Then without warning, she turned her full attention on me.

"So, Oll—um, Liv, I know how persistent Mira can be when she sets her mind on something, so what took you so long? And what were these drastic measures? How did she get to you?"

"I didn't want to jeopardize our friendship or my relationship with Cassie." Tiffany interjected with a derisive little snort, for which Sarah and Megan both elbowed her. "But then Mira got drunk and kissed me." The good friends (as I was starting to think of Sarah and Megan) laughed, and Mira buried her face in her hands.

"That worked?" Megan asked.

"Well, Mira's a great kisser." I couldn't help making Tiffany uncomfortable with information she didn't want (obvious from her squirming in her seat). "So it was working fine until she got sick."

"I think *I'm* going to be sick," Tiffany whispered, and again Mira either ignored or didn't catch her friend's comment.

"It wasn't as bad as it sounds," she said.

"It was probably worse," Megan said. "Like that time with Chip."

"I'm sorry. You dated someone named Chip?" I asked. Mira was blushing adorably, and if we hadn't been at a table full of her recently alarmed friends, I would have kissed her.

"She tried," Sarah jumped in. "But there was a slight issue with food poisoning—"

"Does your mother know?" Tiffany asked out of nowhere. The tentative playful atmosphere we'd built up immediately vanished.

"No," Mira answered.

"Don't you think someone should tell her? Gail should know what her daughter is doing."

"I think that's up to Mira," I jumped in.

"You also think there's nothing wrong with this." She gestured at us, her habitual glower on display. "Mira used to know better. Her mother still does."

"What the hell, Tiff?" Sarah hissed at her.

"Why are you hiding this from her, Mira? Are you ashamed?" Mira stared at her but said nothing. "Or is this not serious? Because if this is just a fluke, some temporary experiment or something, I would understand not telling Gail. Why destroy her for a sick experiment? If that's the case, I can ignore it and forgive you."

"It is serious. I'm not ashamed, and I don't need your forgiveness."

"No, you need counseling."

"I'm confused," I jumped in again. "Mira's been telling me for days that you're one of her best friends, but so far I've seen no evidence to back that claim. You might want to start acting like a friend."

Tiffany looked at me with a frightening blend of pity and scorn. Sarah's eyes darted back and forth between Tiffany and me, and Megan's mouth had fallen open once again, whether from Tiffany's behavior or mine I didn't know or care.

"I only want what's best for Mira, and if she can't see that this isn't it, well, I'll have to try to open her eyes."

"What is that supposed to mean?" I knew from unfortunate experience Tiffany was capable of grade-A bitchery, but for Mira's sake, I hoped she'd lost her flair for malevolence.

"You'll see." She stood and put on her coat. "I can't stay and be a part of this. Call me when you come to your senses, Mira. Don't take too long."

And then she was gone. Megan and Sarah sprang to action to comfort their friend, but it quickly became obvious that nothing would salvage the night. I thanked Sarah and Megan, promised Mira would call them, and then I took Mira home.

She remained silent the whole ride home, but she didn't cry. As the cab sped through the city, she held my hand and stared out the window at the lightly falling snow. Though I had expected something like this (on a much larger scale), I didn't know what to do or say to comfort her. While it could have been helpful to point out how wonderful Sarah and Megan had been, doing so ran the risk of highlighting how awful Tiffany had been in comparison. Mira had honestly expected better of her friends, and learning that Tiffany was the narrow-minded, judgmental shrew I'd always known her to be crushed Mira.

"What if she tells my mother?" Mira asked in a whisper once we made it to her house.

"Is that something she would do?"

"I have no idea. I wouldn't have thought so before tonight, but it's possible." She wiped away the tears that had started falling. "They go to the same church, and Tiffany is always angling to improve her status. Blatant homophobia and misguided concern for me could get her in good with my mother."

"Listen," I pulled her in for a hug. "You don't need to worry about this right now. Your mother is leaving the country tomorrow, so unless Tiffany calls her tonight, you've got some time to figure things out."

"Like how to induce selective amnesia in my mother?"

"Or how to reason with Tiffany."

"Easier said than done."

"You held your own tonight, in the face of your first dose of bigotry. You can handle this."

"I'm not like you. I don't stand up for myself."

"Trust me, honey, you do. I've seen it firsthand."

"Not when it comes to my mother."

"Not yet, but maybe someday you will. In the meantime, we'll look into panic rooms and that amnesia thing."

She sank onto her bed, and I sank beside her. "Tiffany will come around." A bitter laugh was her reply. "You did." At that she smiled, weakly, but it was something. "Until then you're stuck with me."

"More like the other way around." She blew her nose while I tried to figure out what she meant. "I'm so sorry, Liv, for ever making you feel this...ugly and unwanted. I don't know how you can stand to be near me."

"That's what you're upset about?" She sniffed and nodded gently. "Don't be."

"I hate to think you ever felt this bad. I hate more that I was responsible."

"Honey, you make me way happier than you ever made me miserable."

"Really?"

"Really."

"Thank you."

"For what?"

"Being you. Making me stronger."

"My pleasure." I kissed her forehead. "Now, tomorrow is Christmas Eve, the first Christmas Eve I've been excited about in a long, long time, and I'm not going to let Tiffany or your mother or anything else ruin it for me." I unzipped her dress. "We're going to go to bed, and I'm going to hold you until you feel better."

"Will you still hold me even after I feel better?"

"I'll hold you always."

CHAPTER TWENTY-THREE

We almost didn't get the family Christmas I'd been looking forward to, thanks to some festive but extreme weather. The snow, so light and harmless the previous evening, continued falling throughout the night and increased in intensity. We woke on Christmas Eve to half a foot of snow with more coming down steadily, and we were sure of two things: one, we'd have a white Christmas, and two, any kind of commuting would suck.

As a committed cyclist and public transportation devotee, I usually regarded a big snowfall with reverent wonder. I never had to worry about driving in it, so I could appreciate the serene beauty of a world covered in snow. But that morning, upon seeing heaping mounds of winter's most loved and hated offering, my first thought was worry over Cassie being stranded with her grandparents. Not that she didn't love them, but it wouldn't be the holiday any of us expected or planned for. And after Mira's disastrous night with her friends, the last thing she needed was the disappointment of Christmas without her daughter.

Mira dismissed my concerns with an uncharacteristically head-in-the-snow approach to dealing with problems.

"She'll be here," she said, frowning at the sideways blowing snow. "We've always spent Christmas together. She'll be here."

"Honey, it's supposed to keep coming down for another three hours. At least."

"And then the plows will come out, the streets will be cleared, and Cassie will come home. Count on it."

She spoke with such confidence and determination that all I could do was agree and try to figure out an alternate plan in the event the meteorologists had also been optimistic and naïve in their estimation of the storm's eventual end.

Mira had the good fortune of going to work to distract her from the weather and the possibility that Christmas with Cassie would be delayed. I, on the other hand, had been forced to take the day off, so when I wasn't discovering the futility of shoveling her porch and walkway in the midst of a near blizzard, I was exploring transportation options for Cassie. By noon I had devised three viable backup plans to get Cassie from Winnetka to Mira's house (none of them quick or easy), but as it turned out, my scheming was as pointless as my shoveling. The snow stopped falling just after noon, and though it continued blowing about in frigid, swirling eddies that obscured vision and slowed already plodding traffic almost to a standstill, as Mira predicted the plows cleared enough of the roads to allow Cassie and her grandparents safe (albeit slow) passage—a trip that normally took about forty minutes had lasted close to two hours.

"They made it!" Mira called out when she saw Cassie hurrying up the walkway to their house.

She pulled her daughter in for a tight hug as I helped her grandparents haul in Cassie's luggage and several large packages. Though I probably should have been hiding again, we'd been monitoring the sidewalk for so long in eager anticipation of Cassie's appearance on the scene that, in my excitement over her arrival, I forgot about subterfuge. Good thing, too, as Cassie's possessions had more than doubled in her brief time away. It seemed wrong to leave an older couple to struggle with so many large and cumbersome boxes and bags. I wondered if they'd rented a moving van to transport all of Cassie's Christmas spoils.

"Thanks for your help. I don't believe we've met. I'm Cassie's granddad, Clifford Morgan." Mr. Morgan shook my hand, his grip firm but heartfelt. He had that thick, perfectly graying hair that dapper older men seemed to be blessed with, and his eyes crinkled when he smiled. "This is my wife, Ivy." A petite, light blond woman with startling blue eyes, Ivy offered a demure handshake.

"Liv Cucinelli. I'm, um..." I struggled to explain my relationship to Cassie and Mira.

"She's, um..." Mira apparently suffered from the same issue, but Cassie had no problem clarifying who I was and why I was at her house for a major family holiday.

"She's mom's girlfriend," Cassie informed them and went to hang up her coat.

Mira's mouth opened and closed a few times, but no sound escaped. I was no better off, but the Morgans remained unfazed by Cassie's revelation.

"It's a pleasure to meet you, Liv," Ivy said, her smile broad and genuine.

"Cassie's told me wonderful things about you both," I managed to sputter out, but Mira still said nothing. She looked pale and dangerously close to passing out. I moved to escort her to a seat, but Ivy Morgan came to the rescue.

"We're happy you aren't alone, dear," she said before pulling Mira into a hug. When Mira finally relaxed into the embrace and her in-laws' acceptance, I wanted to hug Ivy, too.

"Can Grandma and Grandpa stay for dinner?" Cassie asked when she rejoined the adults.

"We couldn't," Clifford said.

"Of course you can, Cliff. We'd be happy to have you. I'm sure you'd appreciate a break from being in the car." Mira hesitated briefly. "And it would give you all a chance to get to know one another better."

"We would love that," he said, and he looked like he genuinely would. "But we have dinner plans with our nephew and his partner, and thanks to traffic, we're already running late. We need to get going."

"But we would like the chance to know Liv better," Ivy said and again offered a sincere smile. I already loved this woman. I wanted her to be *my* grandmother. "Maybe we can all have dinner sometime while Cassie's on break from school."

"Of course," Mira said. "That would be wonderful." And after a flurry of pleasantries (for me), hugs (for Cassie and Mira) and Christmas wishes (for all of us), they were gone.

"Why did you do that?" Mira's eyes flashed as she addressed her daughter.

"What? Am I not supposed to be honest anymore?"

It was a good question, one for which Mira didn't have a ready answer.

"Liv belongs with us now, and I don't want to have to hide her when Grandma and Grandpa come over. That's stupid," she explained, and I felt a lump creep into my throat at the same time as my eyes filled with tears. This had to be the weirdest, most emotional Christmas Eve I'd ever experienced. "And I knew they would be fine with it."

"That they were." Mira shook her head gently, possibly wondering (like me) if that exchange had actually happened. "But next time, let me be the one to share the good news, okay?" Cassie smiled and nodded. "Then let's go eat dinner and get Christmas started."

Over dinner I learned that the only Christmas Eve traditions Mira and Cassie had established were binge watching holiday movies and (to my surprise) sampling some of the cookies that were supposed to be for Santa. Add to the mix a soft, warm blanket big enough for the three of us to share, and it sounded like the perfect night to me. I said as much, but then Cassie asked what holiday traditions I had.

"Lately, I haven't celebrated the holidays often enough to have traditions." I shrugged, feeling oddly sorry for myself in the midst of the best holiday I'd ever experienced. "Unless work counts."

"What about when you were a kid?" she persisted.

I reflected on the holidays of my childhood. Even with a limited budget to work with, Mom always made the most of our little celebrations. She usually cooked, which didn't happen often during the rest of the year thanks to her hectic work schedule. No matter what was for dinner, we would stuff ourselves and then, weather permitting, walk around the neighborhood or go downtown to see the Christmas displays. Most years we'd end the night playing a board game and eating some kind of dessert. There was only one custom that took place every year without fail.

"We always opened one present on Christmas Eve—I think because I was too impatient to wait and my mom needed something to calm me down."

"Then we'll do that, too," Mira said and looked to her daughter for confirmation. Cassie eagerly agreed.

"You guys don't have to change how you do things just because I'm here." I was touched by their willingness to modify their customs and make me feel more included, but the fact that they'd invited me to celebrate with them was more than enough.

"Are you kidding? You're giving us an excuse to start the presents early. Of course we'll do it your way."

"Thank you." The tears threatened again, and that damn lump returned to my throat, preventing me from speaking the words as I signed them.

Mira smiled and held my hand for a minute, and then we all stood at the same time and cleared the table so we could begin the festivities. I'd never seen Cassie move so fast to wash dishes. My dishtowel and I had a hard time keeping up with her. And while she and I restored the kitchen to order, Mira lit a fire, plugged in the tree, set us up with a generous helping of cookies and poured us all festive beverages (some more festive than others).

"How do we do this?" Mira asked once we gathered around the tree, its multi-colored lights competing with the glow of the fire for our attention.

"Mom and I would just pick one present that we wanted to open."

That was all the invitation they needed to dive in and grab a package. I noticed they both picked gifts from me (whether by coincidence or because they knew what to expect from one another, I didn't know), but where Cassie had been lured in by the larger of the two packages from me, Mira had opted for the smaller present. Nervous about how the night would unfold, I picked up the first gift I saw with my name on it—from Cassie as it turned out.

I held my unopened present as they tore through the flimsy paper that stood between them and their gifts. Cassie's eyes widened, and her mouth fell open when she laid eyes on her very own microscope—small, used and not very powerful, but hers all the same. The hug she gave me squeezed the air from my lungs and brought tears back to my eyes, but it was worth it to see her so excited.

I wasn't the only teary one in the room. Mira sat staring at the vintage camera bag I'd picked up in a resale shop. I didn't know if she wanted or needed a camera bag, but as soon as I saw it, I knew it should be hers. Soft brown leather and somehow cool and classy at the same time, it seemed quintessentially her.

"That's not your real present," I said, suddenly terrified that she hated it. "But it made me think of you."

"I love it. Thank you." She hugged me too, more loving, less bone-crushing, but still tear-inducing. This holiday would be the death of my stoic, tough girl image for sure.

"Open yours, Liv." Cassie pointed at the carefully wrapped gift beside me.

I had almost forgotten I was getting presents. It seemed sort of irrelevant considering everything else the day had already brought me, but I could sense Cassie's eagerness to share whatever that box contained with me. Inside I found my new favorite T-shirt—a navy blue crew-neck shirt with the words "Ichthyology Diva" in white. I had no idea where she found it, but I planned to wear it at every possible opportunity.

Cassie made it through *Elf* but fell asleep halfway through our second movie, and though I knew Mira and I had a lot of work yet to do before we could call it a night, I couldn't bring myself to suggest breaking up the party and putting Cassie to bed. She looked so peaceful snuggled against her mom, who, in turn, was snuggled against me. I didn't want to disturb any of us. I ignored the movie and instead studied the cozy family scene before me, committing to memory as much as possible. I sensed this was a turning point for me, and I wanted to hang onto it for as long as I could.

When the credits rolled, Mira tried to wake Cassie. She nudged her, squeezed her shoulder, gently shook her and even slipped out from beneath her, leaving her to flop onto the couch—to no avail. Cassie was out of it. Mira stood, chin in one hand, the other hand on her hip, studying her soundly sleeping daughter and puzzling over what to do. She looked beautifully flummoxed, but gazing at her all night wouldn't fix things any faster than staring at Cassie's slumbering form would. I saw only one solution.

"Let me," I said and lifted Cassie from the couch. "I guess the remake of *Miracle on 34th Street* isn't her thing."

Cassie's head lolled against my shoulder as I carried her to her bedroom, but she didn't stir. My hair fluttered slightly in the breeze from her deep, even breaths, and without even realizing what I was doing, I placed a gentle kiss on her forehead. She shifted then but just enough to cuddle against me more, endearing her to me further and making my ovaries and uterus cry out with previously suppressed maternal desire.

"That kid of yours is something else," I said after we left an adorably sound asleep Cassie in her room. I still hadn't recovered from my brush with maternal yearning, but I was trying to distance myself from it. Playful holiday fun was the order of the night.

Mira, however, looked anything but playful. I couldn't quite read her expression—happiness mixed with something—and it flustered me.

"How do you do that?"

"What?" I asked.

"Do and say everything just right, even though you're not doing anything out of the ordinary, at least not for you." I knew I looked as confused as I felt because she blew out a frustrated breath and tried to explain. "This is the complete opposite of what I thought I wanted."

"Oh," I said, crestfallen and wondering where I'd gone wrong—not even a month into my first real relationship, and I'd already blown it.

"No, it's a good thing. I've been swept off my feet with presents and trips and smooth moves. Cassie's dad was outstanding in that area. Deficient in every other respect, but the wooing he excelled at." I still didn't know where she was headed, and I worried I'd let her down, that I hadn't done or been enough. "But you...You don't worry about charming me with grand romantic gestures. You're just you, in everything you do, and it's perfect."

"I'm hardly perfect." I felt myself blushing, and all the emotions I'd been struggling with all night rushed back to the forefront.

"For me you are. I love—"

I put my fingers over her mouth to prevent her from finishing that statement. "Don't you dare say that."

"Why not?" She looked perplexed and a little hurt.

"I've barely held it together tonight. If you say what I think you're about to say, I'm done for. And I'd like to survive long enough to experience all of Christmas, not just the pre-show."

She was smirking at my ridiculousness. "You know that not saying it doesn't mean it doesn't exist, right?" I was clenching my jaw in an effort not to cry, so I just nodded. "Okay. I'll wait."

"Thank you." I hugged her, holding her for a long time, long enough, I hoped, to let her know that she wasn't the only one feeling an as yet unnamable emotion. "So how do we make Christmas happen?" I asked, still not letting her go.

"Follow me," she said and led me to Santa Claus Central, a.k.a. her dining room.

She assigned me the arduous task of making it look like Santa had enjoyed his cookies, the process of which meant eating said cookies over a plate to catch a convincing array of crumbs, while she wrapped Cassie's mountain of presents in the special, for Santa only paper. Having seen my gift-wrapping skills, she understood that I'd be better put to use as entertainment and cookie disposal. Considering her impressive speed with giftwrap and ribbon, she didn't need much help anyway.

"Cassie still believes in Santa Claus?" I asked after my third cookie, one festively decorated and kind of pepperminty.

"Not since she was six, but there's really no downside to indulging her mother's love of holiday excess." She did some trick with her scissors to make the ends of the ribbon extra curly before adding that package to the pile to go under the tree. "She loves it too. Fair warning, she will barge into the bedroom ridiculously early."

"Is that going to be weird?"

"I don't see why it would be. I'm sure she's figured out where you spend the night every time you're here. Just try not to be naked."

"That could be a challenge." My cookies all gone, she put me to work handing her pieces of tape.

"You're up to it," she said and grabbed the last of Santa's presents for Cassie.

"Is there anything else I need to know about tomorrow? Any important rituals or other clothing restrictions?"

"Be prepared to have your picture taken. A lot. And there's a mandatory mid-morning nap." She put the finishing touches on the gift and then started moving the multitude of presents toward the tree.

"I like the sound of that," I said, right behind her with several packages.

"We're supposed to sleep," she admonished me.

"Party pooper."

CHAPTER TWENTY-FOUR

As promised, Cassie came running into Mira's room just before five in the morning and woke us by jumping on the bed. The gravel beneath my eyelids offered an unnecessary reminder that we hadn't even come close to getting enough sleep, but from Cassie's frenzied state, I surmised our chances of hitting the snooze button for another three hours were nonexistent. On a positive note, her excitement about Christmas and Santa Claus overrode any awkwardness that might have emerged upon finding her mother and me in bed together (clothed, as instructed). Once we sat up and started stretching, Cassie, assured that Christmas was underway, leapt from the bed and darted toward the door, her penguin pajamas an adorable blur speeding from the room.

"Are you ready for this?" Mira asked around a yawn.

"Does it matter?" I yawned back, a new respect for parents settling over me.

"Not even a little." At least she was being honest.

After a brief detour through the kitchen to supply ourselves with caffeine (though Cassie had more than enough energy for all of us), Mira and I shuffled into the living room to find Cassie sitting cross-legged on the floor, her knees bouncing up and down in her excitement. She'd plugged in the tree. Apparently an illuminated fir was an essential component of gift exchanges, and though I feared the blindingly festive glare would sear my weary and sensitive retinas, to my relief, the soft glow of the colored lights made the experience less harsh than I anticipated. Cassie's eagerness further dulled my agony, and I settled in next to Mira on the couch, ready to be swept up by Cassie's overabundant holiday spirit.

Considering her impatience to pounce on the agglomeration of packages for her, I expected her to tear into her presents in a flurry of torn paper and discarded ribbons, uncovering the hidden treasures in about the same length of time it would take a cheetah to overtake a gazelle. My inner conservationist winced again at the waste of it all, but Cassie's ever-expanding smile and Mira's promise to recycle everything recyclable soothed me a bit. To my surprise, Cassie took her time to appreciate every gift she unwrapped. She paused to admire each item and tell "Santa" how much she loved her new book, toy, game or whatever Mira had stockpiled for her. She was such a good kid, and she especially loved the many additions to her library, for which I thought Santa should have considered bringing Cassie another bookshelf or perhaps an additional wing on the house. Though I had nothing to do with her love of reading, I felt oddly proud that her excitement over books surpassed her joyous reaction to the rest of her windfall.

Once Santa's generosity had been expended, we took a small break to snag more caffeine while Cassie tidied up the chaos of her already lucrative holiday. I didn't mind the delay, not only because I was hopeful that another cup of tea would put a dent in my exhaustion but also because I was terrified Mira wouldn't like her present, that it would be too impersonal (though I had tried to personalize it despite my limitations). There wasn't much I could do about it at that point, but in the moment, delaying her disappointment seemed more agreeable than facing the consequences of a bad gift.

It seemed like we'd been opening gifts for a year (in truth it had taken less than an hour), and I couldn't remember half of what had been exchanged, though the image of Mira tearing up over whatever Cassie gave her stuck in my mind. When Mira (already the holiday hero and Cassie's main benefactor) handed out the remainder of her presents, I noted the typically Mom gift of clothes for Cassie, and I could see why, given the opportunity the night before, she'd chosen to open a gift from me and not her mother. Still, she was too sweet not to show almost as much genuine appreciation for her new skirts and sweaters as she did for her fun presents. It probably didn't hurt that Mira had impeccable taste.

I didn't escape the gift of clothing either. In addition to the nicest pair of jeans I'd ever owned (because I look good in jeans, according to Mira), she also added charcoal gray dress pants and a glut of shirts (not one polo or T-shirt) and sweaters to my limited wardrobe.

"For the interview you're sure to have. Now you don't have to shop."

"Thank you."

Appreciating her thoughtfulness, I admired the clothes again, marveling at her ability to find apparel that suited me and still managed to look appropriate for more formal settings than I was used to. I also wondered how she afforded so much extravagance on what I assumed was a salary no higher than mine. It made sense for her to splurge on her daughter, but this bordered on extreme. Even though I appreciated her generosity, I didn't want her to go into debt over me.

At least she hadn't overextended herself on her other presents for me. I was now the grateful owner of *Jaws*, *Jaws 2* and the truly awful *Jaws 3-D* on DVD, which I planned to make her watch with me some night when Cassie would be spared its cinematic wrongs. Then, in my first brush with emotional overload that day, I unwrapped a framed black-and-white photo of Cassie and me. Normally, I couldn't stand pictures of myself, but this one I loved, not just because Mira had taken it, but also because the picture so clearly captured my connection to Cassie, a connection that had quickly become one of the most important in my life. In the photograph a furrowed-browed Cassie held her bottom lip between her teeth and had tucked her hair behind her ear. She scowled slightly at the book in front of her while to her left, I smiled and pointed to some key piece of information. We had been so focused on whatever bit of homework had caused Cassie momentary distress that I hadn't even noticed Mira and her camera.

"I love it. Thank you." Forgetting we had an audience, I kissed Mira then, perhaps with a bit more intensity than was permissible at a G-rated holiday function.

"Gross," Cassie critiqued our display, her expression one of perturbed impatience. "No making out on Christmas. Not before all the presents are opened."

"Sorry," we both apologized, and I scurried to put my gifts into the hands of their eager recipients.

By the time my offerings for Mira and Cassie were the only two unopened presents under the tree, I had run the emotional gamut from peripheral joy through worry and fear to overwhelmed happiness. I worried that, after all the books Cassie had already amassed that morning, one more would be unimpressive, but that was needless fretting on my part. The delicate way she handled her autographed copy of Jane Goodall's *Reason for Hope* and the bone-crushing hug she followed up with told me that she treasured the book. At least I'd conquered Christmas where Cassie was concerned. Her mother was another issue.

Mira sat staring at the open box in front of her, her puzzled expression telling me she hadn't made up her mind yet. When Cassie asked what was in the box, she pulled out empty picture frames, some large, others small, some ornate and some simple, all of them waiting to be filled with her photographs. After my original idea fell through, I'd scoured antique stores and resale shops around the city in search of good deals and had come away with about two dozen unique frames, one of which contained a gift card from one of the few photography stores in the city and a note explaining my reasons for Plan B Christmas.

"I did *not* want to give you a gift card," I had written. "I wanted to give you something so that you could take even more beautiful pictures, but as it turns out, I know nothing about photography and even less about what kind of equipment you want or need. I promise to learn. Until then, this is my attempt to make sure you keep taking photographs. I can't wait to see them all."

I had gone back and forth about how to sign my genius note begging forgiveness for being a terrible gift giver. Certainly it would make a somewhat lame, impersonal gift more palatable if I wrote *Love* instead of *Merry Christmas* or just my name, but that would make my emotions a bit more real than I was ready for (not that the holiday itself hadn't already taken care of that). Also, even though it might take years, I thought that Mira might prefer to hear that I loved her before reading it (a convincing excuse in the moment). In the end, the innocuous, emotionally safer *Merry Christmas* won, but as she poured over what I'd written, I wished I hadn't chickened out.

I was ready to apologize and offer to get her something better when she stood up and hugged me. "Thank you," she whispered in my ear and hugged me tighter. "No one has ever taken me seriously before, not when it comes to this."

"You don't hate it?" I asked.

"I love it. It's one of the best presents I've ever gotten." She kissed me, and this time Cassie didn't interrupt us. She sat on the couch trying to read one of her new books but succumbing to drowsiness.

"Is it too early for that nap you mentioned?" I stifled a yawn.

"Tempting," she whispered, a wicked little half-smile playing across her lips.

"Not that kind of nap, young lady. Cassie and I made plans for later this morning, and we'll all want to be well rested."

"What are you two plotting?"

"Nothing much. We just thought you might like to go ice skating with us."

"What? You guys hate ice skating."

"We don't hate it, Mom," Cassie joined in.

"We just don't like it as much as you do," I explained.

"And we want you to be happy," Cassie added.

"Also, we discussed this back when I thought you might hate your Christmas present, and I figured I'd have to make it up to you." Mira shook her head in a familiar reaction to just how ridiculous I could be. "So what do you say? Do you want to watch Cassie and me make fools of ourselves? You can even bring your camera."

"Oh, there will absolutely be pictures of this."

"Terrific," I groaned even though I was smiling. "But we have four hours before the skating ribbon opens, and I was promised a nap."

Christmas naps, I learned, took place on the couch. With three of us sharing the space, it wasn't the most comfortable for sleeping, but it was cozy. We tested a few different arrangements and finally settled on the same basic position we'd been in the night before with Cassie cuddling up to Mira, who laid against me. I gently stroked her hair as we drifted off to sleep.

"Liv?" Mira said, her voice soft, but still rousing me.

"What?"

"You know that thing you won't let me say?"

"Yeah."

"It's still true."

I squeezed her tighter and kissed the top of her head. "Glad I'm not the only one," I told her and then kissed her again before falling into the most contented sleep of my life.

We woke two hours later to the sound of the doorbell. At first I thought I dreamed it, but then I felt Mira shift and take all of her warmth from me. Cassie was sitting up, too, rubbing the sleep from her eyes. I realized someone must be at the door. Who would pay a call on Christmas morning was beyond me, but whoever stood on the other side of the door was insistent. The lights flashed as the doorbell sounded again, and a perplexed Mira opened the door and blanched.

"Mother," she gasped, and I immediately panicked. I had no time to flee the scene, and there was no way I would go unnoticed. How the hell could we explain my pajama-clad presence on Christmas morning to the dark lord? No matter how friendly and generous Mira was, it was nothing short of bizarre to invite a friend over in the wee hours of Christmas to sit around in pj's opening presents. Without a doubt, Mrs. Mephistopheles would suspect something.

"What are you doing here?" Mira asked. She stood rooted to the entryway floor, effectively blocking her mother's entrance.

"It's Christmas, Mira. Where else should I be?"

"Um, Europe?"

"Are you unaware that we had a blizzard yesterday? My flight was canceled, and rather than spending any more time with the masses at O'Hare, I decided to come here and have Christmas with my daughter and granddaughter. Is that so strange?"

The archfiend pushed past Mira and handed off her coat that I felt certain was made of puppy fur. She glanced around the living room, her expression sitting somewhere between smile and scowl as she surveyed the tree, the presents and her cautiously smiling granddaughter. When her eyes landed on me, she reared back. At least she wasn't the only one who could drop a bombshell.

"You again. Why are you always taking part in my family's celebrations?"

"Mother, Liv is a guest in my home."

While I appreciated Mira's attempt to force civility from her mother, it went unnoticed by the holiday hobgoblin.

"Don't you have a family of your own?"

I do now, I thought, and they would never be my backup plan. But instead of saying what I wanted, I smiled insincerely and offered her more holiday cheer than she could ever hope to summon. "Merry Christmas to you, too, Gail."

"You should have let us know you were coming." Gail's withering glance at her daughter clearly indicated her opinion of Mira's lesson in etiquette. "We weren't expecting you, Mother."

"I noticed." She eyed the jumble of blankets on the couch, and I flinched. Even though she couldn't possibly have seen all of us cuddled together or surmised the homey scene she'd disturbed, I couldn't shake the notion that, somehow, she knew.

"Let me get you some coffee," a flustered Mira continued, seemingly oblivious to her mother's comment.

"What *are* you doing here?" the evil one asked me, and Mira froze, waiting to hear my answer.

"Like you said, I don't have a family, and being holiday orphans themselves, Mira and Cassie took pity on me and invited me to join them. Up to now it's been the best Christmas I've ever had."

"I see," she said and pursed her lips. It seemed like she was trying to make up her mind about something. Maybe she was reconsidering her earlier (correct) assumptions, or (more likely) she was trying to decide if she could get away with showing her true colors by asking me to suffer through a lonely holiday so that she could enjoy a lesbian-free Christmas with her family. "Merry Christmas," she said and swept majestically over to the couch to engage a startled Cassie in conversation. Her back to me, I accepted my dismissal and followed Mira into the kitchen.

"What are we going to do?" Mira whispered.

"Just a guess, but I think we're going to postpone ice skating. Unless you think you can talk your mom into it. She could be hell on ice. Literally."

"Be serious," she hissed.

"We'll be just friends while she's here."

"What if she decides to spend the night?"

"Has she ever spent the night here before?" I asked, trying to picture Gail Butler roughing it in a space under forty thousand square feet.

"No," she admitted.

"Then in the unlikely event that she breaks with tradition, I'll sleep at my apartment." Mira looked crushed, and I wished I could offer her more than verbal comfort. "It's just one night."

"But it's Christmas."

"I know, but unless you want to tell her what's really going on—"

"And unleash Armageddon?"

"You're right. That's really more of an Easter conversation." She glared at me but couldn't hide the hint of a smile that showed up. "For the record, I love when you're frustrated with me."

"Then you must be in ecstasy right now."

"Close," I said. "Come on, let's go play nice. Maybe she'll leave before she and I kill each other. It will be a Christmas miracle."

While we made it through the rest of the day without fisticuffs, nothing about our time together could be considered miraculous. Gail picked at me under the guise of polite interest. At one point she asked what made me want to feed fish for a living, and I could tell she didn't understand or care that there was more to my job than roaming the piers with a fistful of worms. Mira, in her capacity as peacemaker, tried to make things better by filling her mother in on my possible promotion, but Gail remained unimpressed.

Meanwhile I took every opportunity to flaunt how well I knew Mira and Cassie while they acted as referees. By the time Gail left (shortly after the dinner to which her only contribution was a healthy dose of criticism), the warmth and joy of the early morning were long gone. Cassie and I felt drained, but even after we called it a night, Mira, on edge about our surprise guest, paced the bedroom floor, wringing her hands and wondering what to do about her mother. I finally grabbed her and made her sit.

"We don't even know if she figured it out, but why does it matter if she did?"

"Are you serious?"

"Yes, and I'm not just being an insensitive ass."

"You're sure about that?"

"What's the worst thing that could happen if she knows?"

Mira stayed silent for a long time considering the possibilities. "She would stop speaking to me."

"And is that really a bad thing?" She glared at me. "When is the last time you had a nice conversation with your mother?"

"Junior high," she answered.

"And how often do you feel good about yourself after you talk to her?" Her eyes filled with tears, and I knew without her saying anything that "Never" was the answer to my question. "I'm not saying you should hope for an end to your relationship with her, but I'm also not convinced that it would be the tragedy you're afraid of."

"What about Cassie? Doesn't she deserve to have a relationship with her grandmother?"

"I bet if you asked Cassie, she'd choose your happiness over her grandmother. She loves you, and she doesn't want to see you hurt." I gently wiped the tears from her cheeks. "She's not the only one."

A small smile crept across her face. "That's the second time today you've said that thing we're not supposed to say without really saying it."

"Well, it is the best Christmas ever," I told her. "Don't worry about your mom. Even if she does know, what can she possibly do about it?"

CHAPTER TWENTY-FIVE

My pep talk with Mira notwithstanding, I kept expecting the fallout from Christmas to hit. I couldn't believe that Gail Butler, intolerance personified, had bought our implausible "just friends" performance. Even though we'd managed to keep our hands to ourselves, the way Mira looked at me, which I knew was a mirror image of how I looked at her, conveyed nothing that could be confused for friendly affection. Without a doubt, Lucifer's henchwoman had to suspect something—most likely that I was working overtime on my campaign to corrupt Mira. Either she refused to accept that her daughter had fallen victim to a predatory lesbian, or she was biding her time, waiting for the perfect opportunity to strike. Since an earnest and irrational fear of the gay agenda seemed to be the beast's default setting, I felt a chilling confidence in her imminent revenge.

I tried not to dwell on it. I couldn't hope to have any warning of how and when she would smite me, so it made little sense to spend my days in a constant state of alarm. So I focused on work and made the most of my time with Mira and Cassie, including a rescheduled ice skating date on New Year's Eve, but the uncertainty was torture.

Mira, buoyed by our chat and a handful of conversations with her mother (during which the Harpy of Highland Park made no snide comments about homosexuals in general or me in particular), settled into an easy complacency, even dropping her guard enough to mention me and my hoped-for promotion to the evil one. I couldn't believe she'd voluntarily raised the touchy subject of me with her mother. Nothing good could come from that. In fact, in a complete reversal of my earlier position, I now believed that the wisest approach to Beelzebub's protégé was to deny, deny, deny.

The fact that Gail decided to cancel her trip to Europe altogether rather than just reschedule it reinforced my fears that she was up to no good and that we should avoid her at all costs, but Mira thought nothing of it. Having dodged one bullet, she seemed to believe she had nothing more to fear, but of course, she'd never had her life turned upside down because someone didn't like that she was gay. I couldn't contradict her blissful oblivion with that onerous reminder, not only because I didn't want to send her into a worry tailspin, but also because she would assume I still hadn't forgiven her.

Thankfully, once the holidays passed, my anxiety found a new (or more accurately renewed) target in the form of my job. True, I lived in a near-constant state of uneasiness, but the shift in focus throughout the day proved almost refreshing. Just as I reached my limit of fretting over Gail's inevitable vengeance, concern about my unsuitability for the new position took over. At least that came with an expiration date. I would learn soon enough whether I was in the running or if my colleagues had proved more qualified than I was, but the threat of retribution for the sin of loving Mira Butler could hang over my head indefinitely. As long as Mira stayed with me and in the closet, I feared I'd have no peace until Gail died. I briefly considered wishing for a massive coronary to fell my nemesis, but that only killed people with hearts.

Mental turmoil aside, life gradually returned to normal, at least for a while. Two weeks after Cassie's break from school ended, Roman asked to see me in his office. I'd been meaning to talk to him anyway. I still hadn't heard from Cassie's principal about career day. I assumed that meant he wasn't interested in my contribution, whether because he'd scheduled speakers well in advance of her forceful suggestion or because he simply didn't want to encourage thirteen year olds to act as booking agents, I wasn't sure. But that didn't mean I couldn't speak at Cassie's school independent of career day. I wanted to get Roman's feedback about setting up a presentation at Cassie's school and others in the city, a suggestion that surely would reflect well on my commitment to education.

Or it would have if not for the conversation that preceded my opportunity to pitch my idea.

Throughout our meeting, he looked about as comfortable as someone being consumed by a flesh-eating virus. It was like he wanted to delay or completely avoid this discussion, an impression that did nothing to ease the tension that began the second he called me into his office. I wanted to believe that he planned on offering me the promotion without the bothersome ritual of the interview process, but I knew that couldn't be the case. I also doubted he would sit me down face to face to tell me I was in the running, nor would he look like the start of a commercial for digestive aids. As far as I knew none of my colleagues had heard any news (certainly not via an in-person welcome to the pool of candidates), so either I was the first employee to be informed of my chances, or this was about something else. Considering his nervous shuffling of the papers on his desk and his unwillingness to look me in the eye, that something else wasn't about to be pleasant for either of us.

"You're probably wondering why I asked to speak with you," he said after a round of the most awkward small talk I'd experienced outside of junior high. I nodded, certain my confusion and concern showed on my face. "This morning, the board informed me of some . . . developments that affect the aquarium and you."

"Positive developments, I hope."

"Not entirely," he admitted, and suddenly I felt like I'd swallowed a megalith and chased it with a pint of molten lava.

"We received a sizeable contribution—large enough to build another wing if we wanted."

For an organization that relied heavily on memberships and charitable contributions, every penny counted. A sudden infusion of cash, especially an enormous one, couldn't be ignored. "What's the downside?" I asked, knowing it must impact me but terrified to learn how.

"The donor had some concerns over the impropriety of your contact with students—"

"What?"

"And stipulated that the money would be withdrawn if you continued in your capacity as an educator."

"What?" I asked again, still grappling with the meaning of Roman's words. "What impropriety, Roman? I've never done anything even remotely questionable around any of the kids I've taught. You know that."

"I do, Liv, and I did my best to convince the board to reconsider their decision, but we're talking about a lot of money."

"From whom?"

"I'm not at liberty to discuss that."

"So I don't even get to know who's accusing me of unspecified impropriety? Do I at least get the opportunity to defend myself?"

"The board's decision is final, Liv."

"Am I fired?" My voice cracked on the last word, and I ground my teeth to prevent tears.

"Absolutely not." He finally looked me in the eye. "I'm determined not to allow that." Meaning the board had suggested termination but he'd intervened to protect my job. At least for now. "Obviously, I can't allow you to teach any more classes, and as for the new position . . ."

"I don't have a chance," I finished his sentence and dropped my head into my hands. "How is this fair?"

"It isn't," he admitted. "But if we must decide between an individual employee fulfilling her potential or the well-being of the aquarium and all the animals we serve, well, we have to look at the bigger picture."

"Right. The big picture. Of course," I said, barely concealing the bitterness I felt.

"I understand how difficult this must be for you, Liv, and if you need to take the rest of the day to . . . collect yourself—"

"I still have work to do," I said, not at all sure how I'd continue functioning for the remainder of the workday.

"Take some time, Liv. I'll see to your tasks myself."

"Thank you, Roman."

I resisted the urge to run from his office and straight out the door. For over a decade, the aquarium had been my sanctuary—watching bluegills or minnows gliding through the water, getting lost in the beauty of the thousands of animals housed there had always brought me peace. If necessary, a visit with the otters never failed to raise my spirits. But now the aquarium was the last place I wanted to be.

I hadn't made it two blocks from the scene of my disgrace when my phone rang. Even though I didn't recognize the number and wasn't in the greatest of moods, something told me to answer.

"Hello?" I said and sniffed.

"Miss Cucinelli?" As soon as I heard Gail Butler's voice, my nightmare morning started to make sense.

"Perfect," I muttered, wondering who she'd bribed to get my phone number. "With the way my morning's gone, I guess I shouldn't be surprised to hear from you."

"Bad day?" She somehow managed to sound innocent.

"I'm betting you already know all about it."

"Is there anything I can do?"

"You haven't done enough?"

"I haven't even started," she hissed, and the malice in her voice chilled me more than the icy wind blasting my face. "This is hardly the first time I've had to rescue my daughter from her own bad judgment, and I'm not about to look the other way while you drag my family into your depraved way of life. Believe me when I say that you are not up to the challenge of doing battle with me."

"Was there something you wanted, Gail?" I don't know how I managed to sound calm when that was the farthest thing from what I felt.

"I'd like to help you, of course."

"You hate me. Why would you want to help me?"

"So that you'll help me."

"Is this the blackmail portion of the conversation? Because I don't want your money, and other than cash, you have nothing of value to offer anyone."

"I can make your little problem at work disappear."

"Excuse me?"

"If you assure me that you'll no longer assert your sick influence over my daughter, I'll guarantee that there will be no more obstacles to your advancement. Of course, if you insist on being part of Mira and Cassie's life, I'll see to it that you're fired. You'll be lucky to find a job selling fish at a pet store." She paused to let her threat sink in. "I trust you'll do what's best for you and for my family."

I wanted to tell her to go fuck herself. I could feel a profanity-laced invective working its way to the surface, but self-preservation took control of my mouth just in time.

"Count on it."

Hitler's nanny likely assumed I'd submitted to her will, and though I doubted she'd back off without some evidence of my departure from Mira's life, I had no problem letting her believe that was the case. In truth, I had no intention of walking away from Mira, not without a fight. No way would I bow to the demands of a woman who thought she could get anything she wanted just by throwing enough money around. And if my stubborn defiance of the demands of an evil overlord wasn't enough to fuel my rage, my refusal to even consider life without Mira and Cassie did the trick. If only I knew how to fight back.

By the time I reached Mira's house, my anger had dissipated and been replaced by fear and sadness. What chance did I have in a war with Gail Butler, who would barely have to touch her endless resources to destroy little working-class me? This wasn't even a David and Goliath battle. It was more like tadpole and Goliath. If I got lucky, I could find a position at another aquarium, but I'd almost certainly have to leave the state—and my new family. My other option was to accept my oppressor's terms and lose them anyway. Once again my life was at a hopeless crossroads.

"What is with the women in your family?" I barked, startling poor Mira, who was using her day off to catch up on housework. "Why do you keep trying to ruin my life?"

"I thought we were past that," she said, setting aside her dusting.

"We are," I whined. I couldn't help it. I was on the verge of tears, and Mira's sympathy was about to push me into all-out weeping.

"What happened, Liv? Talk to me."

"My boss called me into his office today to tell me about a large donation that the aquarium just received. He didn't tell me exactly how big, but his eyes had that glazed over, fiscally ecstatic look to them, so I'm guessing it was pretty drool-worthy."

She said nothing, but her face was ashen. She squeezed her eyes closed and looked like she was bracing for an impact.

"He told me about it just before he informed me that I won't be teaching any more classes, and I can't be considered for the Educational Director position, per the donor's request."

She sank onto the couch behind her.

"Not ten minutes after I left Roman's office, I got a call from your mother."

"Oh, no." Her expression was a blend of anger, frustration, pain and sadness. "She wields her checkbook like a weapon. What did she do?"

"She'd be happy to rescind that stipulation if I just do her the tiniest of favors and stop corrupting her daughter. So now I'm supposed to choose between doing the thing I love and… being with you."

"I wish I could say I'm surprised, but…For as long as I can remember, she's tried to buy the life she wants for me. When I told her about Cole's affairs, she chastised me for not marrying the senator's son she preferred for a son-in-law. Then she started throwing money at the problem. All I wanted was a hug and some sympathy, not a husband whose temporary fidelity she secured."

I couldn't imagine the hardship of a mother with more material wealth than human emotion, and my heart broke for her.

"She's the same with Cassie. She's been looking into surgery to 'fix' Cassie since we learned she's deaf."

"What?" I momentarily forgot my own anger with Gail in my indignation on Cassie's behalf. "Cassie doesn't want that."

"And the fact you know that after only six months with her while Mother still won't accept what I've been telling her for twelve years says it all, don't you think? She's not concerned with our happiness unless that coincides with what makes her look good. If that means depriving Cassie of one of the most loving, kind and encouraging role models she could ever hope to know just so Mother can be a proud Christian bigot, so be it. And I'm just supposed to let her destroy Cassie, both of us really, because that's what I've always done. She expects me to let her have her way no matter the consequences."

"So what are we going to do?"

"We're going to fix it." She grabbed my hand and pulled me toward the door. "Come with me."

CHAPTER TWENTY-SIX

I didn't know if it was the enormity of the task before us, the daunting hopelessness I felt as I trailed behind Mira or simply my inopportune return to the gaping maw of hell, but somehow Gail Butler's fortress looked even larger than the last time I visited for Cassie's birthday. Thanks to the dreary winter weather, the house also held an ominous gothic gloom as it towered above us. I considered retreating—working at a pet store might not be so bad—but Mira obviously didn't have the same misgivings as I did. Dragging me by the hand, she charged up to the front door and, not even bothering to ring the bell and wait for the maid to escort us in, she barged into her mother's home.

"Mother," she called out as she stormed the castle, easily maneuvering through the confusing chain of vast, mausoleum-like rooms. "We need to talk."

Roughly a mile into our journey through the Butler estate, the hydra herself emerged from one of her first-floor dungeons.

"Mira, dear, this isn't a pep rally. There's no need to shout." She scowled in my direction but otherwise failed to acknowledge my existence. She turned away from us and glided elegantly toward her kitchen.

"Tell me it's not true, Mother."

"What do you mean?" Gail raised a sculpted eyebrow at one of her cowering servants, who, by unspoken command, produced refreshments for us before retreating from the room.

"The hit you took on Liv's career. Tell me you don't need to control me so much that you would threaten her livelihood and sabotage my happiness, not to mention what you're doing to Cassie. You're trying to deprive her of the best teacher and mentor she's ever had."

"Anything I've done has been for your benefit, Mira. I have shielded and cared for you your entire life. You can't expect me to withdraw my protection now." She scowled again, this time at our clasped hands. "Especially when the evidence suggests that you need it more than ever."

"You've protected me, but I'm not sure you've ever shown that you care for me. This is definitely not the way to do it. You need to take it back."

"I'll do no such thing." Gail sipped water from a cut crystal glass. Amazingly she didn't dissolve into a puddle of smoking evil, so I crossed witch off my mental list of explanations for her odiousness.

"You're undermining Liv's career and ruining her life and mine because you don't like that we're dating. Doesn't that seem extreme to you?"

"Ruining her life?" Gail laughed at the thought, almost as if it hadn't occurred to her that her efforts to derail my career would have larger, longer-lasting consequences. "Like any adult, she has a hard decision to make. If she chooses—"

"You've given her the fantastic option of hurting Cassie and me by leaving to preserve herself. That's quite a choice, Mother. Then we're all miserable, but you get your way, and Liv's the bad guy. How can you think that's okay?"

"I'm doing this for you, Mira. I'm looking out for your best interests."

"My best interests. Okay. What do you think they are? To be lonely and bitter forever? Then die alone?"

I was proud of Mira for not throwing a sneering, "Like you" in Gail's direction. Even without a snide reminder of her personality-imposed exile from most of humanity, she recoiled like she'd been slapped, a seemingly natural response from the empress of evil while watching her authority over her daughter slip away. I could almost see her questioning when and how Mira had grown a backbone. Then she glowered at me as the answer to her question dawned on her.

"Don't be dramatic. Of course I don't want you to die alone." The Chimera of Chicagoland seemed almost gently maternal for about half a second. "But I also don't want you to throw your life away. You'll have other opportunities for healthy, normal relationships, and I can't accept that you'll be happy with an insolvent pervert who seduced you for your money."

"Because she couldn't possibly be interested in me," Mira snapped. "And for the record, I seduced her." Gail shuddered at the thought, a reaction lost on Mira as she unleashed further on her mother, but I was so baffled by Gail's statement that I lost the thread of Mira's subsequent tirade.

What money did Gail mean? I guessed Mira would eventually inherit from her mother, assuming she didn't get herself disowned on my account, but her current standard of living fell far below what Hades' lapdog would deem acceptable. And though we'd never discussed finances, I felt certain I could hold my own with Mira in that area. I didn't earn a lot in my current position, but I'd also managed to avoid much in the way of debt. Oblivious to my confusion, Mira and Cerberus had continued their blowup as if the inspiration for it wasn't standing right there.

"You aren't thinking clearly, Mira, not with *her* around, but if she's gone—"

"If she's gone, you'll never see me or your granddaughter again."

"Holy shit," I muttered, taken completely aback by Mira's commitment to my cause.

"Congratulations." Gail looked oddly pleased.

"On?"

"Being so manipulative and controlling. I didn't think you had it in you."

Of course Lucifer's bedfellow would see it that way.

"I'm not," Mira said.

"You're prohibiting my granddaughter from spending time with me unless I do as you say. If the shoe fits." She brushed her hand through the air like a bored magician.

"I'm not prohibiting anything. If Cassie wants to see you, she can, but she adores Liv. She loves her, and once she finds out what you did to Liv, I'm thinking she'll be less eager to visit you than she is to go to the dentist."

"And how would she find out? Are you going to tell her?"

"Yes. If she asks what happened to her friend, and I know she will, I'll tell her exactly what happened because I don't lie to my daughter, Mother."

Gail's eyes narrowed, her lip curled into a hateful grimace, and she glared silently for what seemed like an hour. Mira's only response was to fold her arms across her chest, a clear sign of her resolve.

"Fine," Gail said. "I'll contact the board and rescind my condition." Her tone, as if she was doing me a favor rather than scrambling to preserve her standing in the family, was grating, but I could accept it if it meant getting my classes back. "I'll tell them to give her the promotion."

"What? No!" I interjected.

"That's what you want, isn't it?"

"By my own merits," I said. "Not because you bought it for me."

"Aren't you noble." Gail scowled at me, obviously more irritated that I'd thwarted an easy overture to her daughter than impressed by my moral position.

"Yes, Mother, she is." Mira grabbed my hand again. "And she'll have no trouble getting that promotion without your help."

"If you and Cassie are as attached as you say, her failure will affect you as well. Are you willing to take that gamble? Are you honestly that confident in this woman's knowledge of fish?" Before the scornful way she said *fish*, I hadn't known how much judgment could be conveyed in one tiny syllable.

"It's more than that, and yes, I am."

Gail glowered at us for another hour-long minute before relenting. "Fine," she said. "Have it your way."

Then, acting the whole time like I was the blessed recipient of her benevolence, she picked up the phone.

After that confrontation, the ride to Mira's house felt like a sigh of relief. I couldn't believe that, after coming close to losing almost everything that mattered to me, I got to keep my job and my relationship. And I still had a shot at the promotion, but the thought of not getting it no longer seemed so dire.

Mira didn't stop smiling the entire time she drove, even when more snow started to fall, causing everyone else on the road to forget how to operate their vehicles. I imagined she felt great, not only because the outcome of the last hour was one hundred percent favorable for us, but also because she'd finally confronted her mother and won.

Once we made it home, I collapsed next to her on the couch. I felt like I'd been awake for three years. This had been the longest day of my life, my mother's death and funeral included.

"Thank you for standing up to your mother for me," I said and let my head fall on her shoulder. "No one's defended me like that in a very long time, maybe ever."

"Thanks for showing me it's possible," she said. "I can't believe it worked. My mother never relents."

"I'm glad she did. I don't know what I would have done if I had to hunt for a new job."

She looked at me curiously then. "You would have picked me over your career?"

"I'd pick you over just about anything. I love you."

I'd been terrified of those three words, certain that uttering them would be the verbal equivalent of volunteering to be a prisoner of war, but it was the opposite. Just allowing myself to finally tell Mira the truth of what I felt was better than almost anything I'd ever experienced. It felt so good I wanted to say it fifty more times before the day ended. The look on her face made it even more gratifying, so I said it again. "I love you."

"We're allowed to say that now?" I smiled and nodded. I thought she'd jump at the chance to say what she'd wanted to say for weeks, but instead she kissed me, one of those slow, deep kisses that curls your toes, grabs your heart and makes you believe in fate and soul mates and happily ever after. "I love you." It was almost as good to hear as it was to say.

She curled up in my arms, and we stayed like that, happily kissing and competing to see who could say, "I love you" the most—until I remembered something.

"Hey," I interrupted our mushiness. "What did your mother mean when she said I was after your money? What money?"

"Well," she said, drawing the word out to about four syllables, like she was afraid I'd judge her harshly or call the whole relationship off because of her net worth. "I'm kind of rich."

"'Kind of?'"

"Well, my trust fund would be enough to sustain a small nation, and then I married a wealthy only child who died before he had enough time to spend much of his money. His parents still consider me their daughter and insist on helping me out with Cassie, even though I don't need their help. I wouldn't be surprised if they made us their heirs. And all of that doesn't even come close to what my mother has and what I'll likely inherit if she doesn't leave all her money to some anti-gay Christian coalition just to spite me."

"So you're somewhere in the 'more money than god' bracket?" She nodded. "Then why do you work? You could focus on photography."

She shrugged. "Most of the time work is fun, and I've made some good friends. Plus, it keeps me busy so that I don't end up like my mother. And I think it's good for Cassie. I don't want her to grow up in some privileged bubble, expecting everything to be handed to her and becoming spoiled, like my mother. I want her to have a somewhat normal home life. For most people, that includes going to work."

"You know, I could be the work as normal home life role model if you wanted. Then you could do what really makes you happy without worrying about Cassie succumbing to the allure of privilege. I could be indispensable in that respect."

"Really?" she asked, her playful tone a match to mine. "You would sacrifice yourself like that?"

"Absolutely."

"I think you're onto something. Cassie could definitely benefit from your example. How soon can you start?"

"Immediately." We kissed then, but before we got too carried away, I had to make sure she understood what I was suggesting. "You did get the part where I basically invited myself to live with you and Cassie, didn't you?"

"Yes." She kissed me again. "And I want to help you start packing now."

"Your mother is going to love this, isn't she?"

"That's a battle for another day." She paused. "Do you ever think we'll get to a place where we can be a happy family? With all of the adults getting along and being nice to one another?"

"I doubt it," I said honestly. "I love you, and I would do just about anything for you, but your mother and I getting along? That's crazy talk. I can forgive your mother, but I'm never going to like her."

She laughed and then smiled knowingly. She whispered in my ear, "Remember when you thought the same thing about me?"

"Oh, crap."

EPILOGUE

Eighteen months later

"She's here."

I couldn't tell if Mira sounded more surprised or relieved at the news. She'd been casting a habitual eye out the front window all morning, seeking visual confirmation that her mother's RSVP hadn't been a hallucination. Gail hadn't visited our home since it had become just that—our home—with Mira and me raising poor, impressionable Cassie in a full-fledged den of lesbianism. To her credit, when Gail learned we'd decided to live in extra sinful sin, she hadn't tried to reverse my promotion or get me fired again. She never sought any kind of revenge for our blatant rejection of her so-called Christian values. She'd merely retreated to her own life with her nefarious cohorts and had shown interest in our lives as infrequently as possible. She didn't even bother to show up when Mira (after liberating herself from her superfluous career in retail) opened a gallery to showcase her work and that of other local artists.

Her mother's absence (a blessing as far as I was concerned) hurt Mira, but she remained hopeful that, given enough time, Gail would come around—*before* the wedding she didn't yet know about, if Mira had her way. I, on the other hand, doubted there was enough time left in any of our lives for the princess of darkness to understand that her daughter being in a happy, loving relationship was a good thing, even if only one gender was represented in that relationship.

Mira hurried out to meet her mother (who was dressed like she was heading to a business meeting, not a barbecue) at her car, and I reluctantly followed, being sure to allow them time for the stiff hugs and air kisses that I hoped never to be a part of. So far I'd successfully avoided even a hint of warmth from my future gorgon-in-law, a record I hoped to keep intact indefinitely. Feeling cautiously optimistic that I might gain a few points with Gail, I offered to lug the bulk of her presents for Cassie to the backyard where Cassie's inelegant (but fun) birthday party was already under way.

"Miss Cucinelli," she greeted me coolly, and I smiled at her minimal progress. At least she was willing to refer to me by one of my names rather than testily hissed pronouns. "Don't wrinkle the paper."

"Of course not. We wouldn't want Cassie to have to tear open wrinkled paper." Mira elbowed me, and through gritted teeth, I added, "We're glad you could make it."

Before Mira forced any more pleasantries from either of us, I fled the scene, and after adding Gail's contributions to the already overflowing pile of gifts for Cassie, I took a moment to check on our guests and warn them about the approaching cold front.

Cliff and Ivy Morgan (wearing obviously expensive but backyard party appropriate attire) entertained Sarah and Megan, who laughed enthusiastically at some story Cliff was sharing. Mira's friends had made it their mission to compensate for Tiffany's continued absence until they could bring her back into the fold. From what I'd heard, she'd made slightly more progress than Gail but still wasn't willing to attend events that included the undeniable reminder that her friend had opted for sexual deviancy. She'd taken part in a couple of girls' nights out, but I hadn't seen Tiffany since my unveiling as Mira's girlfriend. I didn't know if I ever would see her again, and if not for the stress that it caused Mira, I really didn't care if I did. I already had enough obstinate homophobes in my social circle.

Patsy, on a break from working the party, kept Alex company at the grill. As soon as he'd heard the word barbecue, he offered his considerable talents as grill master. We only had to provide the necessary supplies, including grill master approved beer, and Alex promised he would take care of feeding the masses. Considering the demands of Mira's hosting duties and my questionable skills with preparing food fit for human consumption, his offer was too good to pass up.

"The buzzard has landed," I told Patsy moments before Gail appeared on the scene.

She squealed and clapped her hands. "I cannot wait to meet this woman."

"Behave," I warned her.

"Don't I always?" Alex and I both rolled our eyes as Patsy divided her attention between the back door and the gate to the yard, waiting for her first glimpse of evil.

Cassie and her cluster of friends, including a few starry-eyed boys falling all over themselves to get her attention, held court in the center of the yard. But even as the queen of the day, Cassie was still Cassie, and as soon as she saw her mother and grandmother enter, she ran to them and embraced Gail warmly. Satan's sister returned the genuine affection, but as soon as Cassie rejoined her friends, Gail's customary poise, confidence and superiority vanished. Mira was inside the house tending to some last-minute detail, leaving me to make my enemy comfortable.

"I've got this." Patsy laid a hand on my arm to halt my reluctant progress. Then she marched up to Gail and introduced herself. "Let me get you something to drink," she said after their air kisses. "You're not driving, are you?"

"Not for a few hours," Gail answered, and they both laughed like they had a private audience with Ellen DeGeneres.

"Unbelievable," I muttered. With her usual charm, Patsy won over the dark one in under two minutes. Meanwhile it had taken me over a year to get the woman to warm up to me enough to use my name. Still, the easier this experience was on Mira's mother, the easier all our lives would be.

Over the next few hours (thanks to countless glasses of wine supplied by Patsy), a nearly unrecognizable Gail marveled at the convenience of the compostable organic bamboo plates on which we served her grilled meats, potato salad, baked beans and other working-class fare. She joked with other partygoers, complimented her daughter on the "lovely party," and in perhaps the strangest turn of events, she had a semi-civil conversation with me.

To both of our satisfaction, I had given Gail a wide berth all day, but when I went on the hunt for more cake plates, I accidentally came face to face with an equally surprised Gail as she emerged from the bathroom.

"Your friend is delightful," she told me after recovering her composure. "I'm surprised."

"Patsy is full of surprises," I said, resisting the bait for a few seconds. "Wait. Were you surprised that I have a friend or that she's delightful?"

"Both actually," she answered, but her words didn't contain their usual malice. "I expected someone more..."

"Lesbian?"

"Exactly."

I briefly considered filling Gail in on Patsy's open-minded view of romantic entanglements but thought better of it. Hetero-seeming Patsy had already made the antichrist a thousand times more pleasant, and what Gail didn't know couldn't hurt me.

"Oh, well." I faltered and ran a nervous hand through my hair. If we weren't actively sparring, I didn't know how to behave around Gail. She flinched, maybe because she was having the same problem I was.

"What is that?" She stared at my finger. "Are you engaged to my daughter?"

Too late, I shoved my hand in my pocket to hide the ring I was still getting used to wearing. "Mira was supposed to talk to you about that. She was waiting for a good time."

"A good time to tell me my daughter is marrying a woman. That will happen any second now, don't you think?"

Even less prepared for a sarcastic Gail Butler than a civil one, I had no clue what to say.

"Still," she said. "At least I know now. That's something."

I wasn't sure how to interpret the relative calm with which Gail was handling this news, and I dreaded saying the wrong thing and inspiring a backlash of some sort. Just then Patsy swept up behind Gail and saved me for the millionth time. "You look like you could use another drink, Gail. I've got just the thing to put color back in your cheeks. Follow me." Patsy escorted Gail back outside to the coolers, and I escaped to find Mira in the kitchen.

"I think your mother is a pod person."

"Explanation?"

"She found out that we're engaged, and she didn't implode or threaten me in any way."

"She wasn't, by any chance, happy about it?"

"More like resigned with the remote possibility of acceptance in the extremely distant future."

"Interesting. So, would this be a good time to tell her we're thinking of making her a grandmother again?"

"Give Patsy a few more days with her, and she might start requesting little gay babies."

"God, I love Patsy," she said and then hugged me.

"Me, too." My arms tightened around her.

"As much as you love me?" she asked.

For an answer, I kissed her. Her hands moved through my hair as I backed her against the counter, and even though words were unnecessary, I spoke all the same.

"Impossible."

Bella Books, Inc.

Women. Books. Even Better Together.

P.O. Box 10543
Tallahassee, FL 32302

Phone: 800-729-4992
www.bellabooks.com